The Boikk Tree

BY SMO

ISBN 978-1-7355298-0-6

For my Grandparents:
Kenneth, Theresa, Charlotte, & Howard
Your memory lives on.

CHAPTER I

The H'nomi Must Fight

She darted between the battling soldiers, dodging swords and fists, her breathing stifled by the putrid air tarnished with dust and blood from the fray. The sun was high and painfully bright; her eyes scanned for cover as she fled and stumbled, panting and clutching an aching side. Ducking under a pair of clashing blades, she slid past a scanty clump of trampled bushes then staggered against the remnants of a smoldering tree trunk which offered meager protection from the surrounding chaos.

Glancing downward, she winced and pulled her hand aside, exposing an indistinct region of blood spreading across her abdomen. An ominous shadow engulfed her and she gasped, spinning around to see only the immense, gleaming metal form of her pursuer—an enraged earth golem. Eyes narrowing, she tightened her grip on her dagger and lunged toward the golem just as its massive serrated saw-arm sliced down, narrowly missing her, but striking the tree, scattering burnt wood and ash.

Zing! A projectile glinted in the sunlight as it whizzed through the air; the golem roared when the arrow pierced the gears of its neck between its armor plating.

"*Finally,*" she murmured. The golem wavered, seeking its new foe, momentarily forgetting about her. Closing her eyes, she whispered a brief incantation: *Evori Maste Insumre*—after which energy surged through her and flowed outward, surrounding her dagger in a golden glow.

Locking her eyes on her target again, she ran and leapt at the golem, opening a wide gash in its leg with her searing blade. She had to jump and roll to avoid its heavy arms swinging backward in an attempt to knock away the unseen offender. Unfortunately she landed among the soldiers still trying to push back their enemy army, the Entari. This blunder earned her a painful kick in the side that sent her reeling and blurred her vision. Catching sight of her, the golem's eyes glowed a vile green and it raised its left fist to strike.

The fist landed—and the rest of the golem with it, crashing down all around her in a huge cloud of dust after a volley of fiery blasts struck the golem while its back was turned. She was still coughing from the smoke and dirt when someone grabbed her arm and pulled her to her feet.

"Nej! You're alive!" he exclaimed, brushing some dust off her shoulders. Nej began to laugh, then choked, coughing harder.

"You should get back to camp, the healers are overrun, but we nearly have this lot in retreat." And then he was gone, running and firing into the fight. Nej struggled over the steaming metal shell of the finished golem. A figure raced toward her from the other side, startling her by catching her in a tight embrace as she stumbled off the golem's corpse. Nej gasped then groaned as she was dragged along more quickly than she would have liked.

"Hurry, we could use another hand."

"Miinae—"

"The entire tent is full and more are gathering outside, what *were* you doing out here?"

"Miinae, I think I'll need to tend to myself before I look at anyone else."

"Hmm? Oh!" Miinae stopped abruptly and frowned with concern as she studied her friend's torso. "What were you *thinking?!*" she retorted angrily, then pulled Nej along again. Nej gave a little laugh and followed her friend to the healing tent.

It didn't take long for Nej to mend her cut, at least enough to stop the bleeding so she could begin aiding the others under the crowded, sweltering canopy. She moved from patient to patient adeptly, applying salves and herbs or casting little healing incantations depending on the injury. Soon Miinae was beside her again, still scolding.

"I thought you didn't like fighting," she accused in a harsh whisper, then bent down to wrap a bandage around a swollen ankle.

"I don't," Nej concurred. "But someone had to distract the golem before he destroyed our camp."

Miinae finished her wrapping and leaned back toward Nej. "I'm sure Jyu can handle a little mech golem. I don't see why—"

"Greetings, ladies!"

"Speaking of Jyu," Nej murmured as the archer swept through the tent flaps, breezed up to them, and clapped a hand on each of their shoulders.

"Entari are back up on their mountain! May they continue down the *other* side!" Jyu said cheerfully.

"Wonderful," Nej replied with forced enthusiasm.

"How dare you let Nesji go get all beat up by that nasty golem!" Miinae grumbled.

"Aww, sis, Nej was great, as always." Jyu gave Miinae a little nudge, then flipped over an empty crate beside them, sat down, and began inspecting the arrows in his quiver. The tent was beginning to clear out, and the girls continued to heal patients as they spoke.

"You're really too young to be out there anyway," Miinae insisted.

"Sometimes I think you're jealous, Mii," Jyu interjected with a grin. "We get to have all the fun while you're stuck here with the wounded."

Miinae scoffed.

"I am perfectly content in my duties. Though I would prefer my best friend's company here beside me, to worrying about her out amongst rampaging golems and merciless Entari."

Nej smiled.

"I was fine, really. Though Jyu certainly didn't arrive a moment too soon."

"At least I wasn't too late!"

"Jyumara, Miinae, Nesjulin," came the proud, aged voice of their clan's Chief as he entered the tent and joined the trio.

"I appreciate your efforts this afternoon; your unique talents were no doubt vital to our success, both in battle and in the recovery of our wounded. But we have little time to linger, as our enemies are only briefly repelled and we are still in great danger. Miinae and Nesjulin, please see that all our injured are motile, in preparation for breaking camp.

"Jyumara, I desire your council on our next...*modus operandi*," concluded the Chief, who turned and left them again, paying little nods and encouraging pats to nearby patients as he passed. Jyu gave a nod to the ladies, collected his things, and hastily followed after the Chief.

"He needs Jyu's advice; what could be so troubling?" Miinae wondered aloud.

"Well he said he wants us to move out. Maybe he's concerned which route to take. It wouldn't do to trail the Entari footsteps."

"That seems rather obvious."

"Shall we find the answer? We seem to have comforted all our patients."

The two young women, who often served as scouts for their tribe, departed the healing tent, then crept stealthily from tent to tent amongst the brush, working their way toward the Chief's large canopy.

Neutral fabrics flowed in the breeze and rainbows of colorful glass beads intermingled with earth-toned carved wooden baubles clinked harmoniously, forming the exterior of the Chief's quarters. It was the largest and most elegant of all the nomadic lodgings specific to their people, the H'nomi. Their clan moved frequently to avoid various dangers that repeatedly presented themselves. The H'nomi were peaceful gatherers and magic-users, at-one with nature and aspirant of the wisdom that comes from study, patience, and understanding.

Miinae and Nesjulin crouched behind the Chief's tent, concealed by trees and large bushes, listening intently to the voices within.

"They've retreated in the exact path we meant to go!"

"We can move east, instead of north.."

"That leaves us vulnerable in the barrens. No, we're safest within the forest. We will continue north through it but I will need scouts ahead of us, guiding us around any enemies we come across. We must reach Mount Hiito."

Miinae and Nesjulin glanced at each other.

"So we're to follow the enemy?" Miinae remarked. Nesjulin sighed and shook her head in displeasure. She remained in quiet contemplation as they rose from their hiding spot and joined the other members of the tribe who were congregating before the Chief's tent, awaiting his orders.

A hush fell over the tribe as the Chief and Jyu appeared from within the canopy and the Chief began to speak:

"I know you all are weary from today's battle. But we must use the remaining hours of daylight to press onward. The Entari know our location, but we do not know theirs, and this gives them an advantage. Jyumara will prepare scouts to journey ahead and determine our enemies whereabouts, finding a safe course for us. Our object is Mount Hiito, and if we move swiftly, we may reach its base before dark. Let us all move together now toward a new land beyond the realm of these belligerent clans."

Jyu caught sight of Miinae and Nesjulin and hurried over to them following his father's announcement.

"I'd like you both scouting. You're up for it?" They nodded and he continued, "Come with me then, we'll find a few more and I'll share my plan."

Together they found three more young H'nomi who often scouted with them. Nej recognized them vaguely: Nurro, Ptolem, and...Kay? Kalac? she paid them little attention; she and Miinae were more interested in their own conversation, until Jyu said, "Alright, now that we're all together..."

Everyone shifted their gaze to him and waited.

"We'll move in one line, fanned out through the forest, spaced so that we can only see two others at a time—one on each side. I'll take one end, the far west, and Kalac will take the far east. The two of us will have only one person to watch for, but we'll also have only danger on the other side.

"Just move straight through; if you see something dangerous, signal your nearest scouts, and they'll pass the word along. If we receive a signal, everyone will converge on that scout, and we'll discuss what should happen next.

"Signal if anyone is in danger as well, or if you lose sight of one another for too long. We'll keep moving forward and at the sight of danger, pause to redirect the rest of the tribe. Understood?"

With a chorus of nods, Jyu positioned them in a line and pointed out the direction each would start, bearing in mind to keep one another in sight. The scouts left immediately, though the remaining clan members were still packing belongings, loading carts and wagons, and gathering horses and other livestock for their continuing journey.

In this time, the Entari had retreated through the forest and reached their camp halfway up Mount Hiito. After depositing their wounded, the majority grabbed a bite of meat and some fresh water then headed back down, to return to where they had left the H'nomi and perhaps catch them unsuspecting, while resting in their camp, preparing for nightfall.

The Entari had noticed some golems in the forest as they climbed up the mountain, but they managed to pass by unseen. Jyu's scouts also discovered the golems, to the northeast. They had been opting for a northeastern path as the Entari had seemed to go northwest. There was a small stream flowing here, its mouth likely high in the mountains, and two golems were sleeping: a water golem within the stream, its weight creating a pond around it in the soft mud, as well as a fire golem a bit further north in the trees; likely it hadn't noticed the water golem sleeping in the brook. Their liquid-like form made them difficult to see within their preferred habitat of water.

The scouts signalled to one another and met near the golems. Jyu had seen a cluster of creatures, possibly more golems, to the far west, and suggested they try to fight these two, in order to then carry on in this otherwise safer direction. After all, the combination of water and fire, as well as taking the pair by surprise, could prove beneficial to the H'nomi. Jyu ran back to their caravan and informed the Chief of what lay ahead. It was deep into sunset when the entire tribe reached the golems. They set down their supplies and received instruction from the Chief and Jyu on how to attack the golems before them.

"As you may know, fire and water golems have a natural dislike for one another. We will use this against them. The scouts will wake both golems and ensure they see one another. No doubt they will focus on each other first, as we are insignificant in their eyes, in which case we will focus on the water golem, and only once he is defeated finish the fire golem. This is because we have the stream beside us, and can easily subdue the fire golem with this resource."

Once again the scouts went ahead, half moving to the fire golem, the rest lingering by the water. At Jyu's signal they all attacked, from sides between the two golems, so upon awakening, the enraged constructs immediately saw one another and began to fight.

As planned, the H'nomi assisted the fire golem initially, even coating their blades and arrows in oil and igniting them on the fire golem before attacking the water. Mages were especially useful, as the water golem seemed unaffected by slashing of blades or punctures of arrows, but their spells of air and fire decidedly irritated the great elemental.

The water golem continued to swell and spray, giving no indication of diminishing in size or strength. Jyu abruptly shouldered his bow, then weaved in and out of fighters, approaching certain individuals and directing them to the far east side, beyond the water golem.

Once several were gathered, Jyu joined them and pointed at an enormous tree with a wide base.

"I need you to cut that down," he explained. "And it has to land on top of the water golem. We crush him with this, and it'll be all over."

The others nodded in agreement, their faces lighting up a bit with hope for this new plan.

"Make sure you angle it to hit him! I'm going to spread the word to get everyone out of the way—and keep the water golem's attention in the other direction. Any questions?"

The others shook their heads and a couple began measuring and positioning themselves for the perfect cut.

Jyu hurried off to complete his part.

Only those nearest the large tree could hear the dull thud of axe on wood; it was mostly drowned out amid the battle. But everyone was on alert, standing well away from the east side and out of the path of the tree. They wouldn't call an alarm or give any indication when it fell so as not to alert the water golem.

When the tree began to crack, the unusual sound more distinct than that of the axe, a pack of H'nomi standing behind the fire golem bashed shields and shouted and cast crackling lighting spells at the water golem as an added distraction.

Both golems were surprised by the sudden cacophony, and were directed more to that than the tree. Nearby fighters' eyes grew large and they began running west as the tall old tree thundered to the ground, its wide branches catching fire on the fire golem as it passed, while the water golem splashed in all directions, now no more than a puddle slowing soaking into the ground, ripped apart by the great tree.

Several H'nomi cheered, but their celebration was short-lived. No longer hindered by the water golem, and given fresh fuel from the fallen branches, the fire golem was proving a force to be reckoned with. Flailing its burning arms, the fire golem inflicted searing burns on the fighters and the surrounding forest. H'nomi steadily gathered bowls and buckets of water from the stream, as each splash weakened the golem's flames. The process, though slow, seemed to be working. But at the next moment the Entari, having heard the sounds of battle, approached from the west, discovering the fight. They attempted to use the opportunity to attack the H'nomi, while they were distracted by the golem. Unfortunately for the Entari, the golem deemed them all an equal threat, and fought Entari and H'nomi just the same.

So the Entari were forced to fight the golem instead, as earlier that day. Jyu grumbled as he moved away from an Entari archer, who'd been firing at the golem from practically at his elbow. He moved near Nej, who'd been casting healing and shielding spells, saying, "Surely all the clans curse the Zenura."

She laughed. "The ones who created the golems? No doubt you're quite right."

The golems were fierce, hazardous giant mechano-elementals who turned on their creators, escaped into the wilds, then created more of themselves on their own. They scattered across the entire land, spreading out even more so than the clans, as they stayed in smaller groups despite their fairly large numbers.

They had crossed paths with the H'nomi countless times. H'nomi would build up a village for a time, only to have to move when some danger threatened. In this way, the H'nomi had been traveling for years, decades, perhaps centuries; no one really knew for certain—it seemed as though they had always lived as nomads, trying to find the sea, to escape their golem-ravaged land and the warring tribes like the Entari, to build ships and sail away. But they ended up staying within the forests for protection, never reaching their goal. Meanwhile the Entari, a powerful war-loving tribe, wished to rule the land, and regain control of the golems and all the other clans—but their plan was flawed, as they seemed only to fight and kill, rather than gain dominance.

Jyu noticed the fire golem was nearly at an end, shrinking more rapidly with the Entari's help. He addressed Nej again, his voice hushed and barely audible due to the adjacent enemies.

"We're going to have the Entari to deal with very soon. We still need a safe route away from their camp. Grab a horse, ride into the mountains, and find a path for us. We don't want to have to keep traveling around the base, it makes us too vulnerable."

Nej nodded. "I'll find a way."

"Tell a couple others to scout too. We'll need to get out of here in a hurry." Again Nej nodded. She went back to the south, into the gloomy twilight beyond the fight, and collected three of their horses, then, staying behind trees, hidden from the armies, she scanned for other scouts. Not far from her she saw the brothers, Nurro and Ptolem, shooting arrows, perhaps at the Entari more than the fire golem.

Approaching them, Nej passed over the reigns for two of the horses and conveyed Jyu's instructions. They each mounted a horse, Nurro opting to take a northeasterly path into the mountains, while Ptolem doubted the ability to pass the mountains at all and said he would scan east and southeast, perhaps continuing around the base despite Jyu's preference to the contrary.

Nej was left with the northwest. She was fairly certain that was the direction from which the Entari came, so she would have to be extra careful. She suspected the 'boys' wanted to find the best path themselves, and so took the more viable directions, leaving her the one that would prove useless. Still it *would* be useful, she thought, to know the exact location of the Entari camp, as well as any other enemies that might lie in their midst.

CHAPTER 2
A Traitor Is Born

Nej was happy to depart from the fighting. Though she often aided her people as scout and lookout, her primary purpose was as a healer—not a damage dealer. She would swing a weapon and strategize and fight when necessary, but preferred not to. It conflicted with her desire to aid and protect others. So Jyu and his father frequently, kindly, enlisted her to seek out and care for injured, or go behind or ahead of troops to let them know if danger was nigh.

She rode swiftly away from her clan, due north first to get out of sight and earshot of the Entari at the battle, then guided her mount cautiously through the dense woods to the base of the rocky mountain which blocked their path, the same mountain which hid the remaining Entari. Her intention was to see how many more Entari there were, and if any other enemies lingered nearby. The other scouts would learn if anything was flanking or even coming from behind.

The sun was completely gone, though a lingering glow on the horizon helped her see that she was beyond the deeper part of the woods, with the vast dark purple sky stretching out above her and twinkling stars winking into existence. It was eerily silent, and Nej felt her horse's steps were much too loud.

Abruptly she dismounted, sending the horse back to her people. She suspected her clan had defeated the fire golem by now and were starting to push back the enemy. The Entari army, if they retreated once more, could soon be following her path. She would be too easily detected on horseback.

She hurried ahead. Night settled quickly. The shadows had vanished into one large darkness across the land and it had grown cold. Clouds passed overhead, blocking out stars and obscuring the moonlight. In the distance, billowing blue-grey clouds foretold of rain.

The mountain proved a more treacherous and taxing climb than Nej had anticipated. Her people were in need of direction now, and she had been gone too long already, with nothing to report. She had seen no signs of the Entari or any camp at all. She glanced up and down the trail she had been following that traced the mountain's outer edge. Nothing in front or behind. This made Nej nervous. She should have found their camp by now. Maybe this route, which seemed well tramped, hadn't been forged by the Entari.

Instead of continuing along the narrow dirt path, she veered into the bushes, climbing a little ledge through dense trees and foliage, working deeper into the mountain. She smelled smoke. A hint of light showed between the trees ahead. She crouched down low and moved forward slowly through the brush. Beyond the tree trunks she saw tents, arranged on what appeared to be a flat, dusty clearing. It was partially shielded by a sort of very shallow cave in the side of the mountain, and concealed on the other sides by trees and brush.

Nej felt relieved upon discovering, at last, the elusive Entari encampment. She had begun to fear she had gone much too far. Hastily she crept closer, trying to count how many might be there, and estimate how many in their army total.

"That's far enough," a man's voice said in a coarse whisper. Nej froze, knowing the enemy had caught her, and suspecting death was not far away. She rose slowly and turned to look at the Entari beside her. First she was struck by his piercing, bright green eyes; then she noticed the unique twisted gold dagger he brandished. She recalled the craftsmanship of the Entari, how they prided themselves in their arms and armor.

The man stared at her in silence, and, as he did not immediately harm her, she began to feel less afraid. At last his eyes narrowed and he pointed his dagger at her.

"A spy," he accused, his voice cold.

"I'm afraid so," she admitted breathlessly. In as far as his people were concerned, this is what she was, though her people really wouldn't wish to fight the Entari—preferably, to find a way around them. But he likely wouldn't care about that. Someone called from the camp, "Captain! ...Korr? Are you out there?"

The man looked toward the voice, gave a small sigh of annoyance, and made a quick decision.

"You'll find spare tabards over there," he said, gesturing toward a rocky inlet built up with a few planks, beside a row of tents. "Put one on—no one will know the difference." She began to reply but a pair of soldiers was fast approaching. She heard footsteps from another direction as well; the Entari were returning from battle, behind her.

Realizing she didn't have time to speak—nor could she find any words to say—she nodded, still in shock, and went to the makeshift armory, which stood empty other than a small torch and several pieces of gear. She heard...Korr, speaking with the men. "Yes, that was one of our scouts reporting. The others are beginning to return. Prepare to mend and sate our comrades."

Korr approached Nej after they had gone. She looked at him uneasily.

"Will you follow my orders?" he asked.

"I will," she agreed at once, too surprised to consider otherwise. He eyed her a moment, then turned and walked back to the center of camp. She knew she was beyond lucky. Why he didn't kill her or capture her immediately she couldn't understand. She supposed this was a type of capture—was she to serve the enemy?

The Entari army was filtering into the camp, and the thought of being amongst the enemy terrified Nej. What if she was discovered? She lingered in the shadows, trying not to be seen, listening to their conversations.

Nej overheard them saying they would need their entire squadron of soldiers the next time as, because of the golems, they had been unable, yet again, to defeat the H'nomi force. The Commander was particularly annoyed by their failure. She stormed into camp and strode straight into her tent, snapping the flap back angrily. That glimpse was more than Nej wanted of the creature. She was a hard, fierce woman, tall with pale skin, sharp features, and long, sleek dark auburn hair pulled back from her face into a high ponytail. She wore elaborate silvery plate armor with crimson lining and a long burgundy cape. She seemed cunning and ruthless, and Nej began to understand why the Entari fought with such ferocity.

Thankfully not all the Entari were so severe. The man who'd discovered and spared her, who all the others referred to as Captain or Korr, was second in command. She wished he was the leader; she felt she might be able to confide in him and earn his understanding.

Nej managed to stay out of sight as the army sat down to dine; she was an experienced scout, despite her recent unfortunate detection, and was able to explore the camp silently while the majority were gathered around the bonfire. She found the infirmary: a large canopy where a few dozen soldiers lay injured and uncomfortable, and certainly not noiseless. She approached hesitantly from the rocky mountain wall at the back of the tent, trying not to draw attention, approaching a soldier isolated in the corner. He glanced up at her, but didn't seem surprised by her presence.

"Ello miss, are ye a new medic?"

She recalled she was wearing one of their tabards. Korr was right, no one knew the difference. She nodded to the soldier.

"Ken ye do anythin fer ma leg?"

She moved around him to get a better look. It was a wonder he had made it back up the mountain. She had struggled a bit herself and hadn't a gash like that.

"Was it the golem?" she asked, then realized she probably wouldn't have been there. But he didn't question it.

"Aye, those earth 'uns 'er mighty strong. I'd wager they're the toughest of 'em all!" Nej knew this wasn't the case—earth were stronger physically than fire, but probably the easiest to defeat after that. It was helpful, admittedly, to stay at a distance. Rather than reveal her golem intel, she gave a little smile of acknowledgment, then stretched her hands out over his leg and focused. Her brow furrowed as her concentration deepened; a white glow emanated from her palms and the soldier made a little sound and asked uncertainly, "What're ye doin?"

She pulled her hands back and smiled at him. "How is that?" He looked down and moved his leg back and forth. A grin played on his face.

"Hey, that's mighty good! Some magic ye got there, I'd like ta learn a spot a that!" She smiled and nodded. Not many could do what she could, even among her people. Of course the H'nomi were more apt at magic, as the Entari shunned it in favor of swords, believing magic was unstable and inefficient, even weak. While her people practiced all sorts of magic, few could harness curing power. Nej typically tried to hide the extent of her ability, as people often got angry if they learned she was a healer and yet could not heal *them*. There were things even magic could not achieve. But anything a healing root or herbal remedy could do over time, she could do as well—and much faster.

She worked her way through the injured, mending as many as she was able, though the work was strenuous, even more so than climbing the mountain! And this was *her* craft! A few seemed beyond any help and it was a wonder they had been brought back at all. She advised them to rest, did what she could on their minor injuries, and found some herbs among the foliage nearby to help with other problems: illness or fever or discomfort she couldn't cure, perhaps because it wasn't clear exactly where it was coming from.

All the soldiers seemed surprised, initially, by her abilities, but didn't question her presence. Some would playfully remark "You aren't like the other medics" and "How did you learn to do that?" but were happy enough with the results that they made no complaints. She worked for two or three hours, until most of the patients were fully recovered. She had just finished mixing and distributing the last of her herbal droughts, hoping she could now get some rest, when Korr arrived.

"You're a healer," he stated bluntly. She nodded. Even more quietly he said, "More useful than I expected. Though also, more questionable. Myra is not fond of magic." Nej guessed Myra must be the Commander she saw earlier. Now she was even less eager to meet the woman.

"We're heading back to the battleground now, as we've rested and you've mended so many additional men—" he paused, considering. "You're coming with me."

They trekked down the mountain in silence. It was the middle of the night; the moon was high in the sky, illuminating their path, until the rain clouds overtook it, just as they reached the base of the mountain. The grass was damp and the air chilly; the fog of their breath mingled with an eery mist lingering over the remains of the previous evening's fight.

The H'nomi were asleep, and in the darkness and mist, their watchers didn't see the enemy soldiers creeping up on them. After defeating the golems and driving back the Entari once more, the H'nomi had made camp to await the return of all their scouts and rest for the night, intending to sojourn on in the morning with fresh spirit. Nej would have felt extreme guilt to know her absence was part of the reason they made camp so soon, without first moving farther away from the Entari and the golem-infested region of woodland.

Rain began to fall as the Entari positioned themselves throughout the camp. When the first bolt of lightning brightened the sky and threatened to reveal the intruders, one Entari gave a shout, which mingled with the echoing thunder, and they all struck at once, slashing tents and guards. Weapon-wielding H'nomi emerged, startled, from their dwellings and tried to fight back, but most were overtaken by the vicious Entari.

Nej stood in the midst of the fray, staring, numb, stunned by the destruction around her. With each flash of lightning slanting through the trees and filtering through the mist, she saw her people falling, wounded, struggling to escape the Entari blades.

She felt helpless, unable to save her own but unwilling to assist the Entari. In her indecision she knew she was failing her people. She shivered in the rain; the water obscured her vision, making her surroundings look all the more dismal.

A crash of thunder shook her from her stupor. Blinking and wiping water from her eyes, Nej surveyed the damage briefly then hurried to the nearest victim. As she knelt to help the fallen H'nomi, a mounted figure galloped into view. She looked up against the rain and recognized Korr. Naturally he wouldn't want her to heal her people. He drew a bow and arrow, and she wondered if he planned to shoot her—or the fallen man? She rose and stepped away from the man, then heard a familiar voice behind her.

"Nej?"

Nej turned toward Miinae, smiling in spite of herself in her joy and relief at seeing her friend, unharmed. Then her face fell as she remembered. With a sidelong glance back at Korr, she gave a little bow to her friend, an incline of her head, but as she lifted her eyes she saw something; an archer in the treeline, aiming at Korr, who was now aiming at...Miinae?

"No!" she yelled, stepping defensively in front of Korr. He glared at her, believing she was trying to prevent him from firing at the H'nomi girl. In that moment he was enraged that she would turn on him after he had spared her life. But as he began to fire, Nej held out her hands and a rippling pale blue barrier swirled into existence, the energy extending up from her hands until it disappeared with a pop! as both Korr and Jyu's arrows struck it simultaneously.

Korr sat motionless as Nej lowered her hands. Nej looked back to her friend, and beyond her at Jyu. The siblings were stunned that she protected the enemy; likely they hadn't noticed Korr firing as well. Miinae looked confused and disbelieving; Jyu, clearly furious, might have retaliated, but the tribe was overrun with Entari soldiers, and the H'nomi were forced to flee. Miinae turned and raced past Jyu, who pulled an injured comrade to his feet then helped him away into the trees.

Nej sighed and faced Korr, who gazed at her with interest before turning and riding off in the opposite direction to aid his fighters. Her people disappeared into the woods while their camp was ravaged by the enemy. When the fighting had ceased and Entari were carelessly rummaging through the tattered remnants of the battle and gradually heading back to their own camp on the hillside, Korr sought out Nej again. He dismounted and offered his horse to an injured comrade before approaching her silently.

Nej stared dejectedly across the ruins, devastated and guilt-stricken at the injury, damage, and even death caused by the Entari. Korr's voice startled her.

"I'm sorry I doubted you," he said. "How did you know?"

Still overwhelmed by the damage to her people, as well as their reaction to her and subsequent departure without her, she absently remarked, "He always seeks out the leaders—especially mounted ones, as they have an advantage." She smiled, thinking of Jyu's tactics. "He'll watch until he can catch one off-guard—" Suddenly she realized the details she was providing might not be quite loyal to her tribe, and quickly finished, "His name is Jyu. He's…a friend." She gave a regretful sigh. Was he still a friend? But he must understand—she hated to see *anyone* hurt, even enemies, and besides, she owed Korr her life.

It was as if Korr read her mind: "Seems we're even now. And it seems you will be *very* useful, with your knowledge of the enemy." She started at that. She still considered the Entari the enemy.

"What's going on here?" Nej went rigid at Myra's sharp tone. She cast her eyes downward, hoping Myra wouldn't question whether or not she was Entari.

"Giving orders, Commander," Korr said immediately.

"I've been instructing our medical personnel to be sure all our wounded are accounted for," he added.

"Mmm," Myra's lips were pursed and eyes narrowed as she studied Nej.

"No need to pass on such an important task," she said suavely, turning to Korr. "You may see to that personally, Captain," she finished, with a somewhat flirtatious smile. She gave a little toss of her head, dismissing him, and Korr bowed curtly before moving swiftly away to rejoin the scavenging soldiers.

Nej looked up as he withdrew and caught his eye momentarily, but Myra drew her attention by stepping closer, towering over her. As their eyes met, Myra said with distrust, "I haven't seen you before…" She slowly circled Nej in scrutiny.

"Then again I don't pay much attention to weaker members of my army." She stopped slightly behind Nej and whispered coldly, "A word of advice: stay away from the Captain. He's mine." She then strode past Nej, taking care to bump roughly into her shoulder, knocking her down into the slippery mud.

Nej stared with a mixture of repulsion and dismay after Myra, unsure why the Commander held her in such contempt—or what to do about it. Nej picked herself up and slowly returned to camp, staying far enough behind the others so Myra wouldn't notice her again.

Back at the Entari camp, she entered the healing tent, where she hoped she would be safe from Myra. She was, at least, safe from the rain, and was grateful for a place to dry, being completely soaked. The storm was less violent now but the rain still fell, and most soldiers had gone straight to their tents. Nej went about healing the wounded again, though there were fewer than before and none were so injured as when they fought the golems. She finished much faster than the first time, and, with the majority of the camp already sleeping, she sought a place to retire for what little of the night remained.

As she looked across the camp, she felt again the guilt that here she was, healing the Entari, when they had just spilt the blood of her own people below.

She was unhappy with her choices: her decision to save herself by aligning with the enemy, and her election to continue to serve and protect the enemy over her own people. She thought of Jyu's expression when she thwarted his arrow. Had she let it hit its mark, she would have been free of Korr. But not free of her own conscience, which told her she owed Korr much more than saving him from a single arrow.

While she still felt indebted to Korr, she was desperate to speak to her friends and try to set things right with them. She could leave now, while everyone was asleep. The thought of sleep almost made her wait a few hours before sneaking away, and she wished she could speak to Korr first—perhaps he would listen, and understand that the H'nomi were no threat; perhaps he would spare them.

But there was still Myra. She would never agree to make peace with any clan. And Nej wouldn't want to put Korr at risk by urging him to bring up the topic. Besides, according to Myra, Nej was no longer to interact with Korr. Without Korr, Nej had no purpose amongst the Entari. No reason to remain. Now she was isolated from her closest comrades among these people and her own.

She stole away stealthily to the armory, where she removed and returned the Entari tabard she had borrowed. Moving into the secluded area behind the armory where the horses were stabled, Nej considered them momentarily, but opted for a quieter means of travel by foot, even if a horse would be quicker. She hurried into the dark, damp forest, beyond the warm glow of the Entari campfires.

She didn't get far.

"Where are you going."

Nej gasped in surprise, wondering how Korr could have possibly noticed her leaving. She turned to face him, considering her response.

"I wish to return to my own people, Sir."

He stepped closer to her, and she gulped.

"I cannot bear watching my people fall," she continued softly, "and being unable to aid them."

"You are a traitor. You'll be killed if you return."

"I am not a traitor!" she burst out, then, looking anxiously about, quieted herself. "My people...will understand," she reasoned, but there was doubt in her voice. She recalled their expressions during the battle and wondered if they *would* understand.

"I can't let you go." He drew his vicious-looking dagger. She stared at him in disbelief. He shrugged. "Your expertise is invaluable. You could turn the tide of this war in our favor. I can't allow you to return to the enemy." She frowned.

"My people are hardly your enemy. We have no desire to fight you—"

"Irrelevant," Korr interjected dismissively. "We aim to conquer all."

"Then why do you take no prisoners?"

He eyed her slyly. "Because they only try to escape."

Nej sighed, almost smiling at his humor despite the gravity of the situation. There was an energy between them, she could feel it. Perhaps he felt it too; maybe that's why he hid her among his people.

"I would not attempt to go," she chose her words carefully, "except the Commander has ordered me away from the only Entari I trust." She met his gaze. "You spared my life. I would remain only to show my loyalty and gratitude to you." She thought to herself, *And to try to convince you to spare the H'nomi.* He smiled and slowly sheathed his dagger.

"If you'll follow my orders, then forget about the Commander."

"You won't get in trouble? Has she not given similar instructions to you?" He laughed. She felt uneasy as he drew nearer. She hastily added, "I won't overstep my bounds; the Commander will have no cause for concern—"

"Are you sure?" he asked, moving closer, then leaned in and kissed her briefly. Taking her hand, he escorted her to his private tent, saying, "You'll stay with me."

CHAPTER 3
The Traitor Returns

Late the next morning, the Entari were preparing to move out, but they needed to scout ahead first as golems were prominent throughout the mountains and the surrounding woods. Nej and Korr were still in Korr's tent, where sunlight made the inside glow warm golden through the tanned hide walls. Korr was about to go meet with his soldiers, when Nej softly requested, "Korr, please allow me to scout ahead."

He gave a little laugh.

"You already ran away from your people, and last night you tried to run from me. Why would I trust you to go off on your own?"

"I didn't run away from my people—"

"I never really bought that you were a spy," Korr interrupted.

"You were rather easy to find—*twice*," he emphasized, "And the fact that you joined with me so readily suggests you weren't very loyal to your people to begin with."

Despite her exasperation with his remarks, Nej had to admit Korr was right—he *had* discovered her far too easily. She took a calming breath and tried to clarify the facts for him.

"When you found me, I wasn't running away, nor was I really spying on you—I was looking for a safe escape route for my clan. You see we are peaceful, and wish to fight no one."

Korr chuckled.

"And I accepted your offer because," she looked at him. "Because, what other option had I."

He smirked, but simply turned to exit the tent. She continued, "You trust me enough to keep me here, but not enough to let me go?"

He paused on the threshold.

"What would happen to you if the Commander found out who I am?" she asked at last. The answer came after ample hesitation.

"I would be killed," he replied in a whisper, unmoving.

"I will not betray you," she promised.

He looked back at her, considering, then nodded in assent.

She gave a nod back, smiling gratefully, then rose and followed him out the tent.

There they parted ways; Korr strode to the center of the camp where soldiers were already gathered, sipping hot drinks against the cool morning air in their cave-like camp, while Nej slipped behind the tent and continued off to the northwest, staying out of sight. One reason Nej wanted to scout was to be away from Myra and the Entari for as long as possible; another was because, contrary to Korr's opinion in light of recent events, she felt she was a decent scout and wished to prove it to him; and lastly, she still hoped to gain useful information for her people, in case she ever got the opportunity to rejoin them.

She made her way down the northwest face of the mountain, which was densely forested. At least the sun was warm and bright, even when filtered by the branches and leaves. She reached a steep drop on the western side and had to veer north; picking her way through the sunlit trees, she came across a rock ledge jutting out of the mountain. Crawling out onto it, she estimated her position as halfway to the base; she also had a clear view across the empty lands beyond. There wasn't a thing in sight but dirt and dry grasses.

Directly below her, however, in the bit of scrub between the wooded mountainside and the desert, was a trio of air golems, hovering and churning, looking much like tornados.

Taking one last glance around, she slipped into the woods again, and retraced her steps back toward the camp. It was easy to do; she had taken the clearest path, and for sure there was no better route to the base of the mountain than straight into those golems. The cliffs were steep to the west and far north, but there seemed to be a trail continuing down from the ledge—as if it may have been traversed before. She should have scouted further, just to be certain the path continued to the base and that no other enemies were lying unseen within the woods below.

But air golems could move suddenly, unexpectedly, and with great speed; it was possible they could move up the mountain and invade the Entari camp before the army cleared out, considering that the path she found may even have been etched by them. She had to return and report her discovery without delay.

As she navigated through the forested mountainside, Nej considered the various routes the different clans had traversed over the years. How they circled around, wasting so much time. Likely it'd been so for generations, due to the constant conflicts sparked each time clans or golems crossed paths. This time the Entari had come from the southeast, and her people from the southwest, but both clans intended to circumnavigate this great mountain and continue northward.

Because the Entari had scattered the H'nomi and dwindled their numbers, they were no longer giving chase but moving on with their plans, believing there to be a camp somewhere north of Mount Hiito which they meant to conquer. Rumor had it that this camp was friendly with golems. Perhaps it was the missing Zenura tribe.

Nej knew her people, typically after an attack, would find a safe, hidden location wherein to build a temporary village, and stay for years, isolated, trying to replenish their numbers and their spirit. She thought, if they did this again, she would have to find them soon, or risk not finding them at all.

At last Nej arrived back at camp, and saw Myra at the center among the soldiers, fairly surrounded, while Korr was speaking to a small group off to the side. Myra saw her, but Nej hurried to Korr. It crossed her mind that no one here had formally introduced themselves, though she had discovered how they were called anyway.

"Captain," she said gently, "There are three air golems in our path, just at the base of the mountain."

"Only three?"

"I believe so; I saw three, and their camp was small. But I will not guarantee that there are not more beyond my sight. I simply sought to warn you as quickly as possible. I will return and bring back more detailed information." He smiled slightly.

Nej smiled back, but her smile disappeared as Myra approached. Myra stepped in front of Nej, pushing her aside, and addressed Korr.

"Report," she demanded.

"Air golems were spotted in the direction of our intended course, Commander."

"And your plan?"

Korr hesitated as he attempted to conjure a solution that Myra would approve. Nej cautiously stepped around Myra and said "Begging your pardon, but, may I offer some insight?" Before Myra could reply Nej turned to the soldiers and began a brief lesson in air golems.

"We do not often encounter air golems, fortunately, for they can be the most challenging to defeat…" The soldiers were drawn to Nej's words and listened attentively. Somehow Myra was equally enthralled, or perhaps momentarily stunned by Nej's audacity.

Nej continued, "They use predominately, if not solely, magical attacks and guile. However, there is a trick to their defeat, and it can be surprisingly simple, so much so that I believe I can solo an air golem successfully. And you can as well—"

"That is enough!" Myra interrupted in annoyance. "How dare you speak as if you are an authority. Soloing an air golem!" She gave a mocking little laugh. "I've learned *you* are a magic user yourself, and I will not have such weakness among my ranks. You are hereby dispelled from service. In fact," her eyes narrowed in suspicion, "I'm not even sure where you came from, as we do not teach magic to our people. Roth, Veriss, take her to my quarters and bind her there, I'll deal with her later."

Nej frowned, meeting Myra's threatening glare, no longer afraid of the bold Commander's unfounded cruelty. She gently lifted a hand to halt the two soldiers who'd pushed through the crowd following Myra's orders, and addressed Myra:

"Commander, I apologize for offending you. I have fought air golems before and hoped my knowledge could assist your soldiers. Forgive me for speaking out of turn, but we all know how dangerous air golems can be—I would hate to see your people die when my experience can help them live."

Myra blinked and her harsh countenance seemed to falter for a moment. The girl's words had sparked a glimmer of respect, perhaps in all the soldiers, as well as Myra.

"Very well," she said at last. "Let's hear your technique. Though I highly doubt it shall be worthwhile." Nej gave a nod of acknowledgement and turned back to the soldiers.

After a minor pause to regather her thoughts, she continued, "Even for magic users, air golems are challenging, because their magic defenses are as strong as their attacks. Yet speed and strength are not so important to defeat them, as cunning. With light and mirrors, a solo fighter can down the air golem. We are often told that sheer numbers is the best method," Nej glanced at Myra, suspecting that was what she too had been taught, "but with a multiplicity spell, a solo fighter can appear to be a dozen fighters, and beguile an air golem without risking any additional lives."

The fighters nodded and whispered to one another at this revelation.

"In addition, the air golem is dangerous because of the powerful, aimed magic spells it uses. However, these bolts have a narrow range, and by flashing light in the golem's eyes, it will miss, or sometimes not even cast for fear of missing. But you must beware of the golem's wide range spell: a large, devastating, whirling air storm. Be sure to stay out of range, for this storm will pull you into its midst, lift you into the air and thrust you incredible distances. Fortunately, the spell is prepared with a broad gesture and thunderous incantation, giving you a few moments to secure yourself." Nej concluded her lesson and turned to Myra. "That is all I know, Commander."

"You...know a great deal," Myra admitted slowly, then folded her hands behind her back and paced while she strategized. "Unfortunately the methods of which you speak are unavailable to us. I have no magic users among my clan. We would be forced to use our sheer numbers, and our swords and shields will have to serve to deflect the golems' spells."

"Not so M'lady," Nej softly interjected. Myra turned toward her sharply. Nej looked at her hesitantly.

"I can cast the necessary spells."

* * *

Myra was not particularly pleased with Nej's additional magic knowledge, beyond mere healing. More and more she believed something wasn't right about Nej, and that it was highly unlikely she was an original member of the Entari clan. Myra wondered who had brought her in, and who she really was. But now was not the time to be concerned with such things; for now they needed her, and would use her.

Nej suggested she could put one of the golems to sleep; this would draw the attention of the other two.Once they located her and approached, she would cast a multiplicity spell, dodge the first spell the golems cast, then blind the caster and attack with the intent of disabling the golem: knocking him to the ground. At this point, everyone should attack the downed golem first, then the slept one. She would try to keep the third's attention and attempt to disable him as well. At the very least, if the first two golems were removed, the final one would be easy enough for the entire army to finish.

They moved out. Entari were generally noisy, with their clanking metal armor and weapons. They made an effort to move slowly and quietly. Nej stayed significantly ahead of the pack, creeping silently through the brush. She reached a scraggly tree, the last barrier before the golem camp; before the golems would have nothing to do but see her. She drew her slender crystal blade, then closed her eyes, focusing a moment. She hated fighting. But she had to—for Korr. Taking a deep breath, she opened her eyes, furrowing her brow in focus as she stood and stepped boldly forward. The golems detected her immediately and turned.

She murmured some words and thrust a hand toward the farthest golem to her left; he fell immediately in slumber. The others were already chanting their spells. She whipped a mirror in front of her in time to blind one, but the other cast, and she dodged to one side, still getting a sting of the spell against her right leg. She immediately cast her multiplicity spell, and copies of her trailed right and left of her, half encircling the golems. The copies all stepped forward in unison as she moved, and they all lifted a mirrored wrist together, though only hers deflected the next attack, which the center golem had successfully targeted at her.

She reflected the spell and blinded him severely. As he reeled, arms flailing wildly, Nej raced toward him, leaped onto his bent knee and caught one of his arms as it swept past. She climbed the wires and rods, a sort of metal exoskeleton, up to his neck, then plunged her blade into the rotating mechanisms that formed his spine. Screaming in pain he whacked her away, but the gears had been unhinged, and slowly the metal parts fell to the ground. The purplish smoke that had comprised the rest of the golem dissipated with a swift breeze.

Nej hit the ground hard and cried out, bruising in several places from the impact. Her leg was numb with shock and she struggled to get back to her feet. The other golem cast at her, now sure of where she was; she yelped as the blast struck the ground beside her, showering her with sparks. She wanted to crawl toward the forest, toward cover, but lying flat on the dirt, Nej saw the Entari were moving in; she had to hold this golem's attention. She heard it casting again and rolled to dodge but the blow struck her almost fully in the arm; her flesh seared and bled and she gritted her teeth against the pain. The golem was casting again; there was no time to waste—she had to keep moving, now.

She hastily recast her multiplicity spell to protect the others and keep the golem focused on her. This helped her successfully dodge the next bolt from the golem. Finally regaining control of her leg, Nej scrambled to her feet, as the golem began prepping a different kind of spell. The others weren't listening; they weren't ready. She quickly chanted her own spell and released the same time he did; an enormous whirlwind, bigger than the golem himself, came racing toward her and the army behind her, who had made a calculated surprise attack on the slept golem.

Nej's spell swirled in her hands and formed a large shield of energy and air, repelling the summoned twister. The pressure was great, and Nej wasn't sure her strength was enough. She pushed with all her might and at last, the twister began to spin away, directly back toward the golem. His eyes grew huge and he let out a shout as he was engulfed by the vortex and carried off.

Nej fell to her knees, panting, sweat-drenched hair clinging to her skin, coated in dust and dirt, her glowing blade streaked with her own blood. She could barely breathe. She glanced at her injured arm; the bleeding was more than she had first thought. And she had pushed herself too hard with that last spell—she had never before been successful with it, and she wasn't in the best condition to use one of that caliber, against such a powerful attack. Although the others had defeated the remaining golem, they hadn't noticed Nej; they were busy cheering and congratulating themselves. As she collapsed to the ground she thought she heard someone speaking, faintly, to her.

* * *

Nej blinked. It was too bright. She began to lift her arm to shade her eyes, but it felt too heavy and fell back to the ground. She tried to sit up, but winced as pain shot through her right arm. She rolled to the left a bit and managed to sit. Squinting against the sun, she saw she was alone under a small canopy of cloth, tied to a tree...that tree...visions of the battle came flooding back.

She inspected her arm. It was crudely bandaged, the binding stained red, though the wound had mostly stopped bleeding. Perhaps the dry heat had helped with that. A hot breeze was raising dust which caught in her throat. Her eyes roamed about for water, but nothing met her gaze. She tugged the soiled bandages off her arm put her left hand over the wound, closed her eyes, and strained, trying to heal, but little happened, and her hand dropped as she sat breathing unevenly.

They all moved on without her then, she concluded. Perhaps assumed she was too far gone. Left her for dead. And if she stayed here, she just might be.

She didn't mind being rid of the Entari. And she refused to admit she needed help. Suddenly something stirred within her; a chill. She scanned the desert nervously, sensing danger.

Something was coming in the distance. A cloud of dust and shadowy forms from the west. One-handed, she tore a long strip off the canopy and loosely wrapped it as a fresh binding around her injured arm. Then, crouching low, she made her way back toward the base of the mountain, which was abundantly forested and would provide ample cover from the eyes of the incoming clan, whoever they were.

She reached the brush at the edge of the wood and began to move into the trees; she crawled behind a large-leafed boele plant, ripping off one of its broad succulent leaves and crushing it in her hand. She pried back some of her wound dressing and pressed the leaf there, wincing. It was painful but would restore her arm's strength soon. She peeked back through the foliage at the approaching—

"What's this!"

Nej gasped as a hand grabbed her and spun her around. A

knife was in her face and two men glared down at her.

"I...I'm a friend," she stammered. She was weak and groggy, and her eyes were still adjusting to the dark wood. After staring at the men a moment, she suddenly recognized them. "Kalac?" she asked, fairly certain of the name; Jyu's friend, and a fellow scout. The men exchanged glances as Jyu's voice said, coldly, "She's a traitor and deserves to die."

She looked up fearfully and saw Jyu's outline, half-hidden in the brush beyond the others; an arrow nocked and leveled at her.

"Jyu," she tried to move forward but the knife still hovered before her. She clenched her jaw then addressed Jyu again, "Jyu, the Entari Captain spared my life, but I am not a traitor. Please—"

"It is not for you to decide her fate," Miinae interjected sternly, stepping up beside her brother. Her icy glare forced Nej to look away. Jyu lowered his arrow and Kalac eased his knife aside. Jyu remarked, "I thought you were a healer." She looked back at him in confusion, taking a moment to comprehend his meaning, then glanced at her arm and replied, "Yes...I...haven't had an opportunity to heal myself—"

"Too busy with *them*?" Jyu chided.

"No," Nej replied gently, "I was unconscious after a row with an air golem. I don't know how long; I awoke alone, and saw something approaching...so I came here, for protection."

"What's coming?" Jyu said, stepping forward, suddenly on the alert, forgetting his scornful, mocking attitude.

"I could not ascertain," Nej slowly turned and peered through the wide leaves, lifting them slightly out of the way. "It's from the west," she pointed, gazing beyond the woods to where the figures had grown quite large and much clearer. Then she paled, whispering, "Tayuuk."

Tayuuk. Relentless, war-driven, enraged; they were beast-like in appearance as well as nature: large, fierce, and brutish. They lived only to hunt, fight, and eat—even amongst themselves when they couldn't find anything else. Terrifying cannibals—the last thing anyone would want to run into.

"Tayuuk, here?" groaned Kalac. Turning to his fellow scout he joked, "Golems are superior company!" His friend grinned.

"Kalac," Miinae commanded, "Take *her* to the Chief, and warn of what is coming.

"Jyu and Sorren, keep watch here while I inform the other scouting party. Most likely we will retreat and attempt to avoid a fight with this band. They seem particularly large." Nej wanted to object, to stay and observe, but instead silently accompanied Kalac.

When they had moved out of earshot, she requested, "Please, let me go, I'm not a traitor. Let me prove myself, so our people might look favorably upon me again."

After a moments consideration, Kalac shook his head. "Sorry, Nej. I don't want to be seen as a traitor myself," he chuckled uncomfortably. As they reached the Chief's hut he added, quietly, "For what it's worth, I don't blame you for tryin' to stay alive." He raised the flap and motioned toward the opening. Nej reluctantly entered, with Kalac following behind.

"Chief," he bowed. "We found Nej at the edge of the forest. Miinae recommended she be brought to you, Sir.

"Perhaps more importantly though," he continued hastily, "Tayuuk are approaching from the West. We require your orders."

The Chief looked with some concern at Nej. At last he addressed Kalac, "We should fall back deeper into the forest. Tell the other scouts to return, and have your party remain at watch to determine the Tayuuk path, in hopes we do not need to move far." Kalac nodded and quickly left the tent.

The Chief gazed at Nej thoughtfully, then turned back to his tables, littered with maps and documents, potions and trinkets. As he tinkered with this and that, he remarked, "You were," he thought for the right word, "Captured," he settled on, "by the Entari," his voice was tight and he spoke with hesitation, as if it were painful to bring forth the words. Nej feared that he would rather have nothing to do with her, perhaps believing she had caused the attack by the Entari, and now had brought the Tayuuk to them as well. She clenched her hands uncomfortably.

"Yes, Sir. I was discovered while scouting for a safe route over the mountain."

The Chief tried to withhold judgment, but he was extremely displeased with the reports he had received from his children regarding her behavior.

"*Why* would the Entari, who attack so cruelly, and violently," he dallied with potions, speaking off-hand, his tone cold, "Why would they spare an enemy scout?"

She struggled to find her voice. "I do not know, Sir. I don't know why he..." Words left her as she recalled the moment she had been discovered, still uncertain what prompted Korr to spare her. Glancing at the Chief, she could see he was still doubtful, but his interest had been piqued, and this gave her confidence.

She continued more boldly, "The Entari Captain ambushed me at the edge of their camp. He instructed me to don one of their vestments in order to blend in with the soldiers. Other men were approaching and, not knowing any better course of action; in fear of the Entari propensity for taking life, I obeyed the Captain's command." The Chief made no comment as he busied himself packing a satchel with his belongings. Nej swallowed, then took his silence as consent to keep talking.

"I healed several of their injured," she admitted. "I'm sorry, I didn't view them as enemies, rather men in pain requiring aid. I told them nothing, except that we do not wish to fight. And I stayed willingly because I thought the other option was death. I thought in time I might change the Captain's views, and bring peace between our clans. I'm sorry if I did wrong."

Still skeptical, the Chief clarified, "You defended the Captain, rather than aiding our fallen, because he had spared your life— and you wished him to continue to do so."

She hung her head. "Yes, Sir, I..." she fought back tears remembering the people she hadn't been allowed to heal that day. At last she softly, but firmly, concluded, "I am glad they left me; that I am free of them. They aren't like us. If only they could desire peace. I don't understand why they are so eager for war."

The chief closed his bag and turned, drawing a deep breath. "I am going to give you a chance. I believe I understand the circumstances, but I am only one H'nomi, and the others may not be so forgiving. If you can earn their trust, regain their friendship, then this incident shall be overlooked." She bowed, grateful for the pardon, though she wondered what the outcome would be if she failed his condition. She supposed she simply must succeed.

"Join Jyu's team monitoring the Tayuuk."

Nej left at once. When she approached the group, however, Miinae glowered and drew her blade. "Trying to escape?"

Nej held up her hands and explained, "Your father has granted me the opportunity to prove I am not a traitor to our people. He directed me to join you in observing the Tayuuk." Miinae sneered. "They have turned away; they are not coming.

You have wasted our time with your false alarm."

Nej frowned, crouching to peer through the leaves, murmuring, "Are you certain?" She gazed out, and indeed, the army was thundering northward in a cloud of dust...but wait. Movement under the canopy—she squinted, and two glowing blue eyes stared back at her. She gasped and reeled backward. "No, they're coming. They know we are here."

"More lies!"

"You may look for yourself, you cannot mistake their eyes, it is a frightening sight—"

"I will not look when I know what you say is false!"

"Miinae," Nej's voice was weary and pleading.

"And to prove it I will stay in this exact spot for there is no danger to be found here!" Nej took Miinae's hands in her own, imploring, "Miinae, in honor of our friendship, please trust me as you once did. Come with me now, for I love you as a sister and cannot bear to see any harm come to you." Before Miinae could reply, Jyu, touched by Nej's words, grasped Miinae's arm and pushed her in the direction of camp.

"Come Miinae, Nej wouldn't lie to us. We must warn the others."

Miinae pulled her arm away roughly and hurried back to camp, the remaining scouts following a short distance behind. As they hastened through the brush, Jyu stayed close to Nej. He whispered, "I forgive you for stopping my arrow." She smiled and placed a hand on his arm, relieved to have his trust again.

They arrived at camp; Miinae had gone directly to the Chief and was just exiting his tent when Nej announced, "The Tayuuk are approaching. We must move out at once."

Miinae scowled and argued, "It's your fault they're coming. You lead them right to us!" Nej, perplexed by the reproach, countered, "Miinae, I did not know you were here when I ran into the woods. You found me!"

Miinae folded her arms across her chest and turned away disdainfully. Nej sighed, adding dejectedly, "And if you wish, I will gladly stand alone against the Tayuuk when they come, if the rest of you will find safety."

Jyu met with his father and conveyed the details of the situation, including the Tayuuk's movement and apparent attempt to fool them. He also dismissed his sister's anxiety over Nej, assuring his father she had no connection to the Tayuuk's sudden arrival.

The Chief and Jyu appeared from within the tent then, silencing everyone. Nej gave them her attention and didn't see Miinae's cold demeanor falter as she glanced at her disheartened friend.

"The Tayuuk wish us to believe they did not detect us," the Chief announced. "They move with unmatched speed; I suspect they are circumnavigating the mountain as we speak, perhaps intending to attack us from both sides, leaving us no escape. It may be too late already."

The Chief continued, claiming that their only option was to retreat, though he was interested in their preference on whether they go North or South—or perhaps split up, with some hiding in the mountain, hoping not to be seen, while others retreated through the forest the way they came from, ideally moving far enough that the Tayuuk wouldn't follow.

But Nej was certain the Tayuuk would continue to pursue them. Whether to go up the mountain and down the other side, or back the way they came, was irrelevant, considering the speed and determination of the Tayuuk. They were artful hunters, and would find and destroy anything once they caught sight or scent of it. There was no question that the H'nomi could not outrun them, so the question became how they could defeat such a great and powerful force. After reaching this conclusion, Nej looked up and approached the Chief to offer an alternative.

"With all due respect, I feel it will be impossible to hide or escape from the Tayuuk. They know we're here. They won't give up. Unless we fight back."

The Chief took a breath, then patiently said, "I am open to suggestion."

Nej spoke quickly.

"I have an idea. Some may think we can't beat the Tayuuk. But I say we can.

"Part of the Tayuuk's strength is that we fear them. Before we even begin to fight, we believe we'll lose, and so we'd rather just run away. The Tayuuk rely on that fear, to make it easier for them to demolish everything in their path."

"Why don't we try to use their tactic against them. We can use magic— multiplicity spells, to give the illusion of greater numbers, and then lay out huge fire waves—hit them hard up front; shock them with unsuspected strength and size. We may not be able to hold out for long against them, but we may scare them enough with our first attack to make them retreat, if they believe we're tougher than they anticipated."

Miinae scoffed, but Jyu said thoughtfully, "I think you have a good point. We can also spread our archers high in the trees and along the mountainside, and fire volleys from every angle, so they think they're surrounded. It just might work, and is probably the best chance we have." Nej smiled at his support, and they all turned toward the Chief for his decision. He was silent and pensive a moment, then nodded. "Those who will not fight, move up into the mountain. The rest, get organized and in position as quickly as possible. At the very least, we can provide the opportunity for some to escape."

CHAPTER 4
The Tayuuk

The H'nomi formed ranks; Nej lead the primary ground assault team. They consisted of hand-to-hand fighters, illusionists, and elementalists. Miinae argued, "She shouldn't lead, she'll get them all killed." Jyu and the archers were beginning to fan out, but he paused to say, "She's the best illusionist, Miinae, and you know it. We don't have that much of a chance anyway. It won't be her fault if the Tayuuk overpower us."

"*Siivar Inil*," Nej said—their blessing protection. A shimmering deep blue glow seemed to flow amongst the H'nomi near her.

As the horde of Tayuuk neared their camp, Jyu gave a signal—flashing a tiny mirror on his wrist—and arrows came flying down upon the massive creatures, beginning the battle. The Tayuuk were taken by surprise: their movement slowed and they looked about in confusion. They were not accustomed to being on the defensive.

Nej led her group silently through the wood, staying low under the cover of brush until she caught the first glimpse of Tayuuk. They wanted to keep the battle within the thickest area of forest, as it would better obscure their numbers and provide greater protection. The Tayuuk were still advancing, though H'nomi archers were picking off a few of their number: some wounded, others spreading out in an attempt to locate their enemies positions.

Giving a shout, Nej stood and cast her spell. Her squad followed suit, and two dozen Nejs along with hundreds of false H'nomi raced toward the Tayuuk from every direction within the woods. The Tayuuk were stunned by the flock racing in and out of bushes and behind trees all around them: some would attack and others wouldn't, most were immune to damage, and there were hundreds; far more than they had expected. While they were distracted by the scattering of foot soldiers, great waves of flame would engulf them, though they couldn't see from whence they came. Were these really the H'nomi?

Nej was in the center of the Tayuuk, her dagger no more than a flash of light in the air as she ducked, darted, spun, and slid amongst the large, muscular, merciless foes. At one point she paused, catching sight of a certain Tayuuk—two glowing blue eyes; it was the same one she had locked eyes with across the desert scrubs. She narrowed her eyes and did a quick swirling strike, downing another Tayuuk. When she looked back, the glowing eyes were gone.

But they weren't gone.

The battle was successful. Nej had several painful slashes across her chest, arms, and back, but she had dealt much worse to the enemy. After a fierce, strong assault, the Tayuuk retreated, fortunately failing to realize that the H'nomi were almost completely burnt out.

The H'nomi were gathering at a new campsite partway up the mountainside to the northeast, and Nej's head was hurting her more and more. During the battle, she kept seeing that one Tayuuk. Eyes staring at her everywhere she looked. It had begun to distract her, though she pushed through, trying to ignore it. Now her head pounded. The Tayuuk were gone but she only saw the eyes. What was this? Could they have discovered magic? It must be a trick; an illusion. She couldn't focus her thoughts. She couldn't focus to heal her injuries. How did he do it?

She fell to the ground holding her head in her hands, yelling for it to stop, and then someone was there, people around her, some asking things, some trying to console her, but there were just glowing eyes... She tried to tell them but everything blurred and grew dim...

Suddenly she opened her eyes and sat up. She was in a tent. But now she saw the eyes again. She hadn't been sleeping, it had just been him staring at her across the desert. And in the woods. And during the fight.

"Are you feeling alright? What happened?" Nej blinked and turned. Jyu was fletching, cutting arrows. But were those eyes behind him? She shook her head, trying to clear it. "They...the Tayuuk, they cast a spell!"

"They aren't magic users," he tried to sound reassuring, though he seemed to doubt his words.

"They must have learned," Nej insisted. "I keep seeing the same Tayuuk, his eyes of blue fire," She broke off and closed her eyes, rubbing her temples. "I can't stop seeing it. And the sound of the battle. He's just staring and they're roaring, he's so calm and still, but they're all around..."

"I think you just need to rest."

"I CAN'T!" she yelled in frustration. Jyu paused, his brow furrowed in alarm.

"I can't," she repeated quietly; forlornly. "It's always there. I need...I need to go, to find them; to make them stop it."

"You can't go to them, they'll kill you!"

"It's the only way," she looked at him resolutely. He gazed back, then sighed and shook his head.

"We'll find another way. I'll talk to my father." He rose and exited. She got up immediately after he had gone and left the tent, trying to sneak away, but she'd barely taken two steps when she was met by Jyu, the Chief, and a couple talented mages; the Chief had already been on his way to visit her.

"I have to go," she began, "The Tayuuk will know how to stop this spell."

"Nesjulin, I understand you are frustrated, and exhausted, but this is not the solution you seek. If this is indeed new magic of the Tayuuk, their intent may be to draw in their prey willingly—evident in your desire to approach them alone, in your condition. You would be no match for their entire army," the Chief reasoned calmly.

Miinae abruptly emerged from the shadows and remarked, "She's probably faking it. Just wants an excuse to leave us again, to tell them where we are, tell them how weak we are now—"

Jyu silenced her with a sharp look.

The Chief sighed.

"I have two of our best mages here. They will work with you to determine if this is a spell, and if so, how to break it."

He escorted Nej back into her tent and left her there with the mages, but she fought her aides and they made little progress. Soon Nej tried again to flee, managing to cast a simple disappearing spell, turning her form somewhat invisible, almost ghostly, and with this guise breezed noiselessly out of the tent.

But the mages pursued her and Nej failed to lose them with no head start. She heard them behind her as she stumbled through the shadowy wood; they were casting spells at her; something struck her and she fell…

The next time she awoke she was in the tent again, but this time tied to the ground with leather wristbands and rope and stakes. Apparently she had struggled hard against her captors, and tried repeatedly to run. But now she couldn't remember any of it, she just saw those eyes over and over. In her delirium, she was uncertain what was real and what was imaginary. She didn't even know the time or the day or how long she had been captive. She pulled and tugged on her bindings. Her arms were weak, her surroundings hazy as her head clouded and pounded at the same time. It was hopeless.

Then Miinae was there. Nej couldn't concentrate. She didn't know what to do or say. "I must go," she must have murmured in her stupor. Did she say it? Or only think it?

Miinae pulled out a dagger. Nej tried to push the images of the Tayuuk out of her mind. What was real? Miinae knelt and cut the ropes holding Nej down. Nej tried to thank her. She thought she managed a nod and a look of gratitude. She wasn't sure what she saw in Miinae's eyes. But she couldn't linger.

It was dark now; the cool night air struck her as she left the tent, clearing her head momentarily. This time her escape was undetected. As she raced through the brush, distinct thoughts penetrated the images still plaguing her mind: How long had she been there? Had it really been only a few hours? Would she be able to track and catch up with the Tayuuk?

She forged through the woods, and then out of the woods, and tried to find signs of the Tayuuk. Which way had they gone? It had been east; northeast? She moved predominantly east across the vast, empty plain beyond the forest and mountains. She ran for some time, and somehow the stillness and solitude eased her aching head.

Sunlight was beginning to lighten the sky, spilling over the horizon, bringing the ground to life. Nej was well into what seemed a sandless desert; dry dirt and occasional blades of brown grass stretched in all directions. She felt safe despite the openness, as she was clearly beyond the sight of any lookouts from her people in the mountains.

However, in this empty landscape, Nej was not entirely alone. As the sun made the land brighter, creating contrast and detail in the earth—the cracks, crevices, rocks, and grass all becoming more defined under the piercing gaze of the sun—Nej noticed some movement on the ground before her. She squinted, then crouched down to see more closely. Was the spell wearing off, or was she just intrigued? A dash of green, then a pair of eyes; the images flooded back, she closed her eyes and shook her head vigorously.

"Ah-ye-ait?"

"What?" Nej rubbed her head, wondering if she had imagined the sound as well. She opened her eyes and looked around. A tiny, "Ahh ye aright?" rose again, from just nearby. She gazed at the little green lizard. He tilted his head at her curiously. "Have you seen…Tayuuk?" she managed, wincing from lack of sleep and food, as well as pain and exhaustion from the spell.

"Tayuuk! Oh they pass ahhwas ago, ye'll nevah catch em!"

"Only…hours?" she mumbled, then had the presence of mind to add, "Which way?"

"That way."

She sighed and laughed half-heartedly.

"Which?"

The lizard darted off to the southeast. "This way!" And he scurried ahead, with Nej stumbling behind as quickly and gracefully as she could manage.

* * *

It happened that the Tayuuk, upon failing to vanquish the H'nomi, had instead struck upon the trail of the Entari. The Entari had moved back east and south after descending Mount Hiito. They had noticed signs of the Tayuuk in the west after defeating the air golems and chose to move swiftly in an opposing direction.

Korr had argued for bringing the severely injured Nej with them, but his protests were silenced by Myra:

"There is little life left in her, and she would only slow us down. I won't have us all fall prey to the Tayuuk on account of one dying healer."

"It isn't right to leave her, right in the path of the Tayuuk! There's still a chance for her if we—"

"Is she so important to you?" Myra snapped.

Korr looked to Myra inquisitively. Did she know?

Myra smirked.

"Oh yes. I am quite certain your little hostage is not one of *my* clan."

It was useless to deny it. Korr attempted to justify her presence at least, to save both their skins.

"She helped us, Myra. We couldn't have—"

"Won the battle without her? Do you have so little confidence in your own people that you think we cannot triumph without the help of one…H'nomi?"

Korr tried to quell his rising frustration and focus on logic before replying.

"It is true, Commander, that we may have defeated the golems without her. But surely at the loss of dozens, or more, of our own soldiers."

"So it is better that one H'nomi life is lost, than many Entari lives. I allowed her to fight with us. She has served her purpose. I am not certain what you hoped to gain by allowing an enemy to infiltrate our ranks; I will humor you that you merely wished to gain intel on the enemy through her, but only by leaving her here now will I overlook your deplorable lack of judgment."

Myra turned and shouted to her soldiers, "Move out!"

* * *

Over the course of the day Nej fought the spell that tried to consume her mind. She conveyed her troubles to her newfound friend.

"Aww, 'tis a bad thing this Tayuuk done! Ta a very nice gi'l, very nice gi'l indeed."

His words brought a smile to Nej's face, and she sought more conversation to try to push away the glowing eyes and the throbbing in her head.

They were on high ground, a sort of plateau southeast of the mountains: grassy, rocky, but still barren of creatures. It was often silent on their world. The animals had moved on in the same way the people were trying to.

"You're the first critter I've seen in…a long time," Nej remarked.

"Yeh," he answered shortly. Nej laughed.

"So what are you doing out here, all alone?"

"Well…" he thought a bit. "Not like sum'n big will come an' make off wih' me. Nothin 'eah! 'Tis a fine place ta be!"

"But…what do you eat?"

"Oh they bugs all oveh; seeds; leaves."

Nej paused. He was friendly, but didn't seem interested in talking too much.

"Do you have a name?"

"Ohh, ye think we jus' like the two-legs, always namin' theh-selves? We don' have family; don' stick togetheh. We don' need name."

Nej frowned. "I'm not so sure that *all* other creatures don't have family or names. Perhaps some simply choose not to. But there's nothing wrong in that."

The lizard chuckled lightly in reply.

A sharp pain stabbed through her head and Nej cried out and fell to the ground. The lizard stopped and skittered back to her. He made sounds of concern.

"This not good…not good, mus' reach Tayuuk quickly."

"What can I do?"

"Ye…ye say ye heal; heal it," the lizard suggested hopefully.

"Hah, I wish I could. It blocks my mind when I try. Don't you see my injuries? I could not even heal those, though I believe others in my clan tried to mend them some."

She sighed, closing her eyes and breathing slowly for a few moments. At last she gave a gentle nod. "Alright. I think it's passing. Let's try to get there; I hope it's not far."

The lizard said nothing but turned and raced onward.

They ran all day, sometimes stopping when Nej felt she couldn't go on or when the spell overpowered her; sometimes she would entreat the lizard to move more slowly for a bit.

"Fasteh is betteh," he would say, then slow his pace so she could walk for a time.

They reached the edge of a forest atop the plateau by evening, as the sun was sinking low in the sky. To the north, the plateau dropped off as a steep, though somewhat shallow, cliff. Nej crouched down at the edge of the forest, and crawled to the cliff and looked down. She gasped in surprise. There was a small camp not far to the northeast at the base of the cliff. She knew the style of the tents and the attire of the soldiers: Entari.

"So they came this way too…how is it that the Tayuuk and Entari are so near one another without realizing it?"

The lizard sidled up beside her, hesitating, noting the urgency in her voice.

"The Tayuuk…they track Entari," the lizard admitted.

"How…" she began, but it was useless to ask how he knew; clearly he was well aware of the goings on of the tribes.

"I hea' the Tayuuk. Neah nightfall they attack; tonight while Entari sleep."

Nej gasped.

"They'll be massacred! With no prior warning… I must tell them."

As she started to rise the lizard said, "The Entari? Oah, the Tayuuk?"

Nej looked at the lizard thoughtfully.

"You're right," she mused, "Telling the Entari is pointless; it may allow them time to prepare for battle, but it's a battle they would lose. The Tayuuk have the high ground and it's too late to change that. No doubt the Tayuuk have watchmen in place…

"Yes, you're right," she repeated, deep in thought as she crept away from the edge of the cliff, then furtively entered the wood, searching for the Tayuuk camp within.

The lizard followed tentatively, at some distance.

The wood was dense and dark. Nej suspected even at midday the sun failed to penetrate far through the branches overhead. The ground comprised of dirt, dead limbs, and fungi. At last she saw a low burning fire—a glow of embers in the dark, and a smoky haze hovering over some dingy, blood-splattered tents. Tayuuk surrounded the fire, eating, muttering, sparring, dozing.

Nej straightened up and strode boldly into the center of their camp. They were too surprised at first to react. But after a moment's hesitation, they began drawing weapons and crowding around their willing victim. She knelt down, awaiting their action, as she was not there to fight. They lifted their weapons to strike when a loud growl erupted from the furthest tent. All turned to watch as the great leader of the Tayuuk bore down upon them.

He loomed over Nej, the dim light of their strange fire casting an eerie glow upon his face.

"You think you're brave, coming here?" he snarled, pacing about her. "You're only a fool to do so," he whispered, then grinned at the crowd. "You know our kind shows no mercy. We yearn only to fight and kill and eat!" At this the others cheered and laughed, eager to get on with their free meal.

"I know of your ways, Sir, though your prowess in arcane arts is either a new skill or well-kept secret," Nej countered.

He chuckled. "Is it not wise to develop additional strengths, to be better adversaries for our many foes?"

"You are wise and powerful indeed, and I have come to implore you to lift the spell you cast upon me. It has caused me constant suffer—" she stopped short and inhaled sharply as she felt a great weight lift off her and her mind cleared. She looked up at him in astonishment, but saw immediately that it was not out of kindness that he had granted her request. His clawed hand shot out and grasped her cloak, scratching her skin in the process, as he yanked her off the ground, drawing her near his greyish fangs.

"What does it matter," he growled, "if your mind is tormented any longer, as your life was forfeit the moment you chose to enter our camp!" With these words he thrust her down roughly and turned away from her.

As she struggled to collect herself from off the ground, Nej replied, "No, Sir—my life was in your hands from the moment your spell pervaded my mind."

As their leader retreated, the others closed in on her, bearing clubs and spears and evil grins, ready to finish her off. Nej hastened to regain the leader's attention.

"Our thoughts are the truest part of ourselves, and a life without freedom of thought, is no life at all."

The Tayuuk tapped their weapons in their hands and drew menacingly closer. Nej's eyes grew wide as one Tayuuk lit what looked like a tattered-cloth-wrapped bone in the fire, swinging it uncomfortably near her skin. Nej forced her gaze away from the impending assault and onto the leader, who had paused, listening.

"In your taking, and now returning, what is most valuable to me, you have my reverence and loyalty. I was, am, and will be your servant."

Nej felt a glimmer of hope when the leader turned toward her again. The other Tayuuk seemed indifferent to her words; one snarled and swung his axe, but a blur intercepted the strike: the leader caught the weapon and thrust it and its wielder backwards into the crowd. The others gnashed their teeth and growled in anger, but the leader silenced them with a glare and a vicious snarl. He grabbed Nej's arm and dragged her toward his tent, leaving the others chuckling and grumbling at their lost feast.

The Tayuuk chief tossed Nej aside within the tent, then settled before a low purple fire where he began etching symbols into the sand and toying with carved gems and stones.

Nej winced as she slowly picked herself up, trying to avoid her many bruises. She observed the chief's work momentarily; could this relate to the spell he'd cast on her? Did he know more magic as well? As fascinating as his foreign magic was, Nej remembered the reason she'd come—not only to have the spell removed, but to save the Entari. She took a deep breath, considering how best to approach the Tayuuk leader.

"Thank you," Nej tried, in a cautious, hushed voice, not wishing to anger or disturb him. He grunted.

"I am exceedingly grateful," she continued, moving nearer, "I fear I can never repay you, though I very much wish to."

He glanced at her, then remarked, offhandedly, "You are the strength of your people." he fiddled with his gems, positioning them in various ways. "They wouldn't have fought if it hadn't been for you."

He looked at her again, his eyes glinting. She remembered those eyes still; likely they would always haunt her from time to time. She whispered, "I only wanted to save the lives of my people."

He chuckled, and continued, "So I targeted you and cast the spell, knowing they wouldn't act without you. And yet you persisted. You succeeded. I am still impressed. But I will learn from this mistake. It took too long for my spell to affect and debilitate you. Either my spell needs adjustment, or you are an exceptional anomaly. Perhaps with you here to test, we shall discover the answer."

A trace of fear swept over her but she pushed it away. Her muscles tensed as she summoned her courage. Regardless of her fate, this was her chance to try to help the Entari. "Use me as you like, Sir, but please, spare the Entari in the camp below."

He turned toward her with a growl of rage and she danced backwards to avoid the wave of his arm as he thrust several sharp jewels across the tent. "Why would I do that for you? My people live for the fight, to feed on their souls!"

"The Entari Captain is my friend," she said gently. "He once spared my life—"

"You have no say over what happens. I could kill you even now."

Nej glanced away, consternation written on her face; the conversation was not progressing as she had hoped.

"With your strength, cunning, and magic, Sir, you are categorically the dominant race on this world. You can easily destroy anyone you choose, at any time. But that is where I appeal to you: You always have a choice."

He growled again, and finally explained, "Out of respect for you, I will enlighten you as to a few truths." She looked to him, intrigued, and honored.

"There is a balance," he began gruffly, "That all the clans adhere to: sometimes, one clan attacks another; other times, a clan is permitted to go. For this enemy, the Entari, it is time to be thinned, and we are the clan to do it.

"We attacked the H'nomi because they were supposed to have been defeated by the Entari—but the Entari had done poorly, and it was all because of you."

He looked at her, again those blue eyes glowing wildly.

"You're throwing everything off. Destroying the balance. Preserving lives that should not be. Breaking ancient codes..." he trailed off, and she took the opportunity to ask, "Perhaps I *am* creating conflict in what is seen as the natural way, but why, why must it be this way? Who decided this?"

"The ancient leaders. The creators of our clans made this determination when we split to seek our own goals. Some of our goals require the destruction of others. And so to appease all, some must die."

His voice became solemn, and focused, as if he was revealing a great secret.

"There is a part in each of us, the leaders, which belongs to something. You," he paused, pointing a finger as he spoke, "You who can upset the balance, who can make leaders refuse to kill, who can make enemies cease to fight; You alone may be able to make it whole again."

She considered this deeply, but before she could ask any more questions, he abruptly said, more gruffly again, "I will spare them as you ask. My warriors will not be pleased. You should go," he gestured toward a second entrance on the other side of his tent, "as they will likely retaliate, and I will not be able to keep them from harming you." With a chuckle he added, "Perhaps not even from attacking me."

Uncertain how to respond, Nej allowed her heart to guide her. Tentatively she approached and briefly wrapped her arms around the great Tayuuk. He was astonished by the unexpected gesture, and before he could react she pulled her arms away, graciously saying, "Thank you, so much," then left hastily as he had instructed.

Her mind was full of the words he spoke, the information given. She felt she must figure out how to do what he had described. Unite the leaders? End the fighting? That he had even suggested she could create change indicated he might be open to it if the possibility were offered to him. This gave her hope. But how could she do it?

* * *

Nej moved stealthily away from the Tayuuk camp, breaking out of the treeline northeast of the Entari. She carefully made her way down the crumbling cliff face, taking advantage of projecting roots and stones. She had to make a significant jump to the ground, which caused stabs of pain in her feet and ankles, and across several lingering gashes in her skin.

She approached the Entari encampment, hugging the cliff to avoid being seen. The darkness helped conceal her form as she neared. Her eyes were searching for Korr.

She didn't see the Captain among the soldiers gathered at the large bonfire, but beyond them she spotted his tent, more to the south, set slightly apart from the other shelters. She managed to move unnoticed through the shadows to Korr's tent and slip silently inside.

"Who—" Korr began, whisking his dagger in front of him as she entered. But he saw 'who' stood motionless before him, and after an initial shock he lowered his blade and more gently said, "You're alive."

She smiled. "I am, perhaps thanks to you," she touched her bandaged arm.

"But why haven't you healed? You look...terrible."

"I must, I am a mess. I have been unable to heal myself, until now." She revealed the Tayuuk's new ability to cast mind-damaging spells, much to Korr's horror.

"How can we fight such an enemy! Myra has been a fool to disregard the potency of magic," he ranted. But Nej soothed, "It's alright—for now, at least. Though the Tayuuk are positioned in the woods on the rise above…"

"What!" Korr interjected.

"It's alright!" Nej insisted. "Their leader has promised not to attack the Entari, at present."

"You've spoken with him?" Korr was incredulous.

"It was their intention to ambush you this night, Korr, but I have dissuaded—"

"With Fier'lor?" Korr interrupted, still disbelieving.

Nej pursed her lips. Was it so impossible to comprehend that she had a civil conversation with a Tayuuk?

"Yes, with the Tayuuk Chief. Is Fier'lor is name? He didn't take the time to give it," she gave a light chuckle. "But he did say he will not attack. Still, I recommend you move out soon, in case the Tayuuk change their minds—or if some fail to follow the will of their leader, though I fully trust his word."

Korr looked concerned, but at last nodded. "You have always displayed sound judgment of character. I will advise the Commander as you suggest."

He moved around her to the tent flap, and paused, turning back. "Remain here," he instructed, then departed.

Nej took a seat on the dirt and began to finally heal her wounds. She hadn't gotten far when Korr returned.

"We're leaving. Myra was…well, she expressed her resentment that *you* were the bearer of this news, so if you could stay out of sight until she calms down…"

Nej nodded. "Of course." As Korr began packing his bedding and preparing to dismantle his tent, she added, "Did you intend for me to come with you?"

Korr glanced at her. "The Commander won't like it, but I think it's best for all of us if you do."

She bowed her head and started to leave when he added, "Nej," and came close, holding her arm. "I'm sorry for leaving you. I'm glad you're alright. And thank you…for intervening on our behalf." Nej smiled and placed her hand over his, squeezed it gently, then pulled herself away. Hurrying outside, she looked for a secluded spot to rest and finish her healing.

Sitting behind some bushes, beneath a small tree next to the cliff wall, Nej at last mended her wounds, and felt enormously better for it. She peeked through the leaves at the Entari packing up their tents. She saw the Commander, shouting orders, looking wrathful and ruthless as ever. Nej leaned back against the tree with a sigh, wondering what she should do.

She didn't want to stay with this clan. She wasn't sure what would happen if she returned to hers. Her people had, after all, bound her and restricted her leaving. At least these Entari had set her free.

She needed information. A place to start. The Tayuuk leader had given her a hint, that something could be done, but he hadn't been very clear. Who could tell her more?

A scuttling beside her drew her attention to her lizard friend.

"Ahh, you're still here!" she said softly, elated to see him.

"Shuh am, Nej." She smiled. "You heard that did you? And so I'm at a disadvantage for I still have nothing to call you."

The lizard scratched at the dirt and swished his tail, but said nothing. Nej let it pass and continued, "I am glad you've stuck around. I especially could use some advice."

"Again? Wha' now?"

"The Tayuuk leader said there is something...inside him, inside all of the leaders—and that maybe I could make it whole again. Do you know what he's talking about?"

The lizard paced a bit, snapping his tail to and fro. "'E tol' ye about...the legen'?"

"The legend? I mean, no, he didn't tell me any more than that. Was he referring to a legend? Because I need to know more. I want to somehow stop all this fighting. He said I could end it."

"Tol' ye tha' did 'e? Hmm...hmmm..." the lizard gazed up at her. "Wondeh what 'e sees in ye eh? Well I s'ppose ye mus' hea' the legen', if ye'h ta make peace..."

Some noises interrupted them—Myra was ordering the army to proceed eastward, following the cliff until it declined. It was still dark, but they were eager to put more distance between themselves and the Tayuuk.

Nej began to wonder how things would have gone if she hadn't interfered, as the Tayuuk leader had indicated. How many times over the decades the clans had fought. How many of their number had been destroyed. So few remained. Soon they would wipe each other out completely. Something had to be done, now.

"Come," Nej said, resting her hand on the ground beside the lizard, who knowingly boarded her open palm. She lifted the lizard onto her shoulder. "Suppose you tell me this legend while we march? I'll hang back so as not to draw attention."

"Shuh, Nej...Lemme think...

CHAPTER 5
The Legend

"This lan' was once beautiful; a utopia. Plants, animals, an' people lived in 'armony, an' ev'yone was 'appy. Lan' always green. Rivehs clea' an' calm. Sun not too 'ot, winds gen'le, an' the sky a vivid blue, even when sky wateh fell.

"Theh weh not *differen'* peoples then. They weh all *one* people. The *H'toshen*. An' they lived beneath the eno'mous *Boikk* tree, laden with lahge, lush, verdant leaves an' giant fruits which gave them all the nourishment they requi'ed. Inna cenneh a' the fruit was a seed, like...like a nut, which they ate as well. An' outside the fruit was a tough shell, that protected the soft, sweet fruit an' the cenneh nut when it fell from the tree...an' until someone wished ta eat it."

Nej smiled. "Sounds like you wish you could eat one."

"Don' innerrupt!" the lizard scolded. Nej bit her lip. The lizard gave a small glare before finding his place again.

"So—theh was only *one* Boikk tree. Its fruits an' nuts, if planned, didn' grow new trees. They weh only ta sustain the H'toshen. Some wondeh'd, an' worried, what should 'appen, if the tree eveh became barren, old, rotten an' dead...wha' would they do then? Eldehs said, *'Don' worry.'* The tree always been theh, an' as long as things weh so, they would all live 'appy an' com-fortably in theh beautiful wuh'ld.

"Buh' this re-assurance was not enough. Some doubt'ed tha' the tree could last eternally. They felt tha' the en' a' theh tree an' theh lifestyle was not jus' a question ah if, buh' when.

"The group a' rogues, 'oo fea'd the tree's ultimate demise, was ratheh small, buh' togetheh they weh trouble. Moah trouble than the othehs anticipated, inna en'. They weh five: Tayuuk, H'nomi, Entari, Zenura, an' Koi'Tan."

Nej's eyes widened as he said their names. The lizard nodded.

"Tha's right. Each rebel founded one a' the clans tha' exist tah-day. Each clan was tuyned an' twisted an' became wha' we now know as unique, differin' peoples. An' each 'ave certain characteristics a' theh foundeh.

"Tayuuk was a lahge, brutish hunteh, fon' ah feastin' on meat, even though the fruit a' the Boikk tree woulda been enough ta sustain 'im. 'E didn' like theh borin' way a livin', an' wann'ed ta fen' for 'imself—hunt 'is own food so 'e could survive even afteh the tree was gone.

"H'nomi was a wise an' peaceful mystic, a Healeh, but in 'eh wisdom she also thought much deepeh than necessary, so much so tha' she doubted the tree's livelihood an' wished ta take mattehs inta 'er own 'ands. Besides, in theh tribe, theh was no need fa' magic, but she enjoyed it; it was powerful, it could protect, it could entertain, it could save life. If theh tribe would not embrace it, she would leave, takin' with 'eh those 'oo shah'ed 'eh beliefs an' special magical talent.

"Entari was a skilled fighteh, likin' ta fashion 'is own weapons an' armor, always preparin' fa' some battle that would neveh come —should life continue in its 'armonious way. 'E wann'ed things like 'onor an' glory; to be rec-anized fa' 'is skill an' dominate oveh othehs through battle—things 'e could neveh achieve amongst theh people. 'E wondeh'd if theh was more out theh, beyond theh lands. Gran' cities filled with people ta fight an' conqueh.

"An' theh weh those like Zenura, a brilliant constructeh, an engineeh, 'oo wann'ed ta build great creatures ta protect 'im; not a tree, but sentient mechanical objects which would bow ta 'is wishes. Ta better 'is people through technology was 'is goal, an' yet 'is creations tuyned on 'im an' almost 'is whole clan was destroyed; those remainin' retreated fah inta the deseht, weh golems 'ave no desi-ah ta go. Rumeh says they 'ave a few golems with'em still that ah' loyal ta theh people.

"An' last–Koi'Tan. She was fie'ce an' intelligent, an' an exceptional, exotic beauty. They say theh isn't any tha' wouldn' mahvel

54

at 'eh featuhs an' form. She felt 'eh looks weh not bein' used ta theh avannage inneh tribe, wheh all weh consideh'd equals. Bein' so lovely didn' gain 'eh any special re-cognition. Too many admi-ahd otheh traits—a person's characteh an' behaviah, oveh theh outward appearance. She wann'ed a clan wheh the beautiful weh admi-ahd above othehs; wheh she was adored an' idolized. An' in the en' she ventured wi' those 'oo shared 'eh beliefs—those with good looks o' those 'oo appreciated 'ehs—ta the equally beautiful yet poisonous jungle ta the south. Whetheh they still live, amongst the wild an' vile jungle creatures an' plants, is unknown.

"Five clans, created by five villains. An' yet, not all fit those categories. Some neveh wann'ed the tree gone, neveh wann'ed life ta change. An' wheh they went, we don' know. Ih's believed tha' as the others depah'ted, joinin' theh new leadehs an' movin' in separate directions, the ones 'oo joined none ling'ahd, an' eventually found a place ta live, or die, amongst the passive crea-tuh's a' the valley."

Nej took a deep breath. So much to take in. She understood how these young, restless individuals could desire more interest-ing and different lives than their tribe, and the tree, could offer. But she was certain that they never anticipated the lingering mal-ady their decision would cause. Somehow, their separating had been a mistake.

"I must reunite the clans, to end this war. Can it be done?"

"Now, now—tha's not the en' ah' the story!"

"Ahh, you're right…"

"An' the legen' may suggest wheh ye should begin." He strut-ted about a bit, licked his 'lips,' and continued.

"Wheh was I—the group ah' rogues, discussed now in detail… Ahh yes, they weh quite determined.

"They weh certain theh woh'ld would tuyn upside down eventually. In due couhse the tree, like all livin' thin's, would die. An' why wait. They weh all prepah'ed ta fen' fa' themselves now, an' wann'ed ta prepah' theh people as well, an' allow them all ta choose whicheveh path—follow whicheveh a' the five a' them they prefeh'd, an' then they could all go theh own separate ways in the lands. The conquereh could conqueh them now an' then, the hunteh could 'unt the othehs now an' then, an' all get theh fill a theh own ways a livin', because peace wasn't enough fa' them, an' besides, it couldn't last fa'eveh anyway.

"So they made a plan. They each used theh special talents

ta create somethin' ta destroy the tree. One built a golem, one a great sword, one learn't the magic a' fiyah, one created poison… An' late one night, while the othehs slept, they attacked the tree, damaged it, eventually cut it down, an' in the cenneh theh was somethin'…an' they split it, split it five ways, an' each took one part an' carried it away with'em.

They say those pieces ah passed down through the leadehs a' each clan; that the leadeh *always* carries it. Gives 'em poweh, but also reminds 'em wheh they came from, an' why they continue on theh journey. No one knows what it is—o' what it was. They say some saw somethin', an' it was glowin', bu' when it was split it went dark, an' no one 'as eveh seen it since, except those five, an' the leadehs 'oo succeeded 'em."

Both the lizard and Nej fell silent for a time. To Nej it was heartbreaking, considering how badly these five desired destruction and hardship over peace and comfort. Perhaps the five were right: *that* many people, with such diverse ideas, couldn't possibly live in peace forever. And after centuries of living separately and fighting, why would they go back? The years apart had strengthened their differences and their mutual dislike. Even if some, like Nej, did want to return, rebels might again ruin it for the rest. A few ruined happiness for so many.

Nej mused, "Why should I try to bring us back together, to live in peace, when others will just try to destroy that harmony over and over again?"

It was a rhetorical remark and she was surprised when the lizard replied, "Right ya ah, why should ya. Peace might be whatcha want, but it ain' wha' anyone else wants. They wanna fight an' kill an' 'unt, an' be 'unted, an' do anythin' they please like spoil't children. On top a' that, *Yoh'* wantin' everyone ta live togetha peaceful, is no differen' from *Theh* wantin' ta be at odds. An' 'oo is ta say which is betteh."

"But I can't have what I want as long as they have what they want. Why did they have to destroy the tree? Why couldn't some have stayed with the tree, while the others left to live how they preferred?"

"Why indeed. Could be, they needed ta destroy the tree in ordeh fa' othehs ta follow 'em. Elsewise, they'da gone off alone without any clan, 'cause 'oo woulda joined as long as they 'ad tha' tree. People don' like change, an' they don' like risk, an' they won' take chances if they don' 'afta." The lizard shrugged, if a lizard can shrug.

"So do you think, if one could gather all five...pieces—fragments—and put them together...?"

The lizard shrugged again. "Can'ey be put back togetheh? An' what ah' they?"

"I want to try," Nej resolved. "All the clans have their following now. They can go be what they want to be. But those who want peace may now have a chance to return to their home and be happy and free again. They may not have spoken up loudly enough back then, and I don't know why, maybe because they didn't expect anyone to kill their tree..." she sighed. "But even if it takes forever, or even if I never solve this mystery, it's an adventure, and it's worth pursuing."

"Tha's the spirit!"

"I should probably start by talking to the leaders, trying to get the fragments from them. But the Tayuuk leader didn't just *give* it to me...so likely the other leaders won't either."

"Why didn't he? Maybe he doesn't really want peace? But he believes change is possible. I'll just have to convince him and the others the time really has come.

"I think I need to learn more."

She looked to the lizard. "Do you know where the Boikk tree stood?" The lizard seemed to smile.

"Lemme see... Ih's said inna lih'l song:

> 'Neath Sunrise Shadow,
> Wheh flowehs fly free,
> Hugged by the Oxbow,
> Grows the Boikk Tree."

She gave a sigh. "Well it sounds beautiful. But that's a nice little riddle isn't it. Besides, so much has changed since then," she murmured on unintelligibly to herself, trying to decipher the little tune. The lizard closed his eyes as he hung carelessly over her shoulder, yawning as he began to drift...

"No, it makes no sense." The lizard popped open one eye at Nej's outburst. "Sunrise shadow? Because the sun really makes it darker," she continued sarcastically.

"Is sunrise now," the lizard noted sleepily.

Nej glanced to the east, where the cliff had finally diminished into a gentle slope, dotted with trees that blocked the sun from view, though the sky was beginning to lighten. Her eyes moved to the soldiers marching before her, partially shaded by the cliff.

Nej blinked, and a shiver ran through her, her eyes growing wide with understanding. She pictured herself beneath the little tree after the air golem fight. It had been west of Mount Hiito; in the morning, it had been shaded.

"On the west side of a mountain, near…near a river. An oxbow, a bend in a river." She pondered. She couldn't recall seeing anything like that. Mount Hiito hadn't had a river near, only narrow trickling streams. And the west side was an arid plain, perhaps once lush grassland or even a lake, but no more for it was desolate, drying—dying. Everything seemed to be so; to be withering away. No wide rivers, and certainly no flying flowers. She sighed and glanced to her friend.

"Any more hints? You seem to know everything."

He grinned, propping his head up on one spindly hand as he gazed up at her. "I 'ave no legitimate bearing fa' this belief, but I always thought the Boikk tree woulda grown somewheh inna cenneh a' the continent. Theh neveh was any mention a' oceans in any vey'sions a' the tale. Maybe the firs' people neveh traveled far enough from the tree ta reach the seas. No need!"

"That's a wonderful start," Nej agreed. "Interestingly enough, my people were headed for the ocean. And I think the other clans are going that direction as well. Everyone wants to escape this place."

Nej frowned. "Seems remarkable that after all this time, not one clan has ever ventured so far as the ocean."

"Strange," the lizard murmured. She glanced at him, but he had closed his eyes again. She stopped moving and looked about, deciding which way to go.

"My people had been moving north and west. Now we've headed mostly east. So I guess fairly due south would be generally the right direction? How big *is* this continent. I hope I don't have to walk for the rest of my life just to find where the tree was! I might still need to find my way back to all the different leaders after that!"

The lizard grunted lightly.

Nej dropped further behind the group, casually moving southward until she disappeared into the forested hillside, well east of the ridge where the Tayuuk had been resting.

CHAPTER 6
The Zenura

The wood was less dense in this area; the dappled sunlight warmed the ground and filled the forest with a golden-green glow. Nej felt great peace in the beauty and solitude, and thought of how it could be this way always, for everyone. No fear of fighting and death. No relentless traveling, on and on with no sign of ending.

Sudden movement caught her eye. A small family of deer was moving through the trees ahead; a mother and a pair of fawns. They were following a narrow brook, heading southwest away from her.

They paused now and then, looking back at her with their large, dark eyes. She cautiously ventured toward the stream, keeping some distance from the animals so as not to spook them.

The land opened into grassland to the southeast, but the trio continued to follow the winding stream south, where it bordered the wood.

The sun rose high in the sky and Nej became aware of how hungry she was. She hoped these animals might lead her to something edible.

In the warmth of the sun, her lizard friend had fallen asleep on her shoulder and gave no indication of waking. She wished to confess her surprise at seeing another animal species, and learn from him if he had in fact come across this place, or these creatures, before. It seemed she would have no such opportunity at the present.

The wood became more exotic, with plants and ferns forming an extravagant oasis. Pushing apart some broad, succulent leaves, Nej stared down into a beautiful pond teeming with wildlife. She had never seen so many animals, or colorful flowers, or such clear blue water. This hidden grove was surely one of few remaining sources of life.

Though Nej stood motionless, relishing in the paradise she had encountered, the animals sensed the presence of a stranger and, in a few moments, the pond became eerily silent. Slowly, the animals began whispering to one another. Nej heard, "You lead her right to us!"

The doe Nej had tailed retorted, "Twas my desire to do so, twasn't by accident—" But she was then interrupted with, "She'll destroy our home, as her kind did before!" The doe scoffed, but others were already rallying in fear.

"We must not let her bring more!"

"Take her down as she would do us!"

As their voices grew in volume as well as hostility, Nej stepped forward to try to soothe them. "Please," she spoke softly, "I am not here to—"

But her words were drowned out by the stampede, and buzz, of all those gathered: deer, mice, squirrels, frogs, and countless insects and birds charged upon her. Nej gasped in surprise and managed to cast a shield spell to protect herself from the initial assault. Her lizard friend awoke startled; he shrieked and leaped from her shoulder, scurrying away to the safety of the tall grasses.

Nej called for him to wait, but he didn't wait, and the momentary distraction caused her to fall prey to the rioting creatures. Insects swarmed her from all sides, stinging and biting, and she struggled to repel them without squishing them to death. So too she attempted to defend herself without harming the small mammals that nipped at her ankles.

As they fought, she tried again to speak: "I am not here to destroy your home!"

She was backing off now, thinking if she could not convince them, she must simply run away.

"Nor to harm you," she continued.

The animals had begun to notice she wasn't truly fighting back, but they didn't seem to care. Nej was knocked to the ground, and she covered her head with her arms as the assailants enveloped her.

As quickly as it began, the attack ceased. Nej slowly lowered her arms and rose to her feet, prepared to flee, and saw the animals attention trained on the woods beyond the pond.

Following their gaze, Nej saw a rustling in the brush, then a large-antlered, white-faced buck emerged from the trees. As he approached, the other animals backed away respectfully.

Nej gave a small bow to this ancient one, clearly a sort of leader amongst these animals, and said nervously, "I did not mean to intrude. I am not your enemy. I wish to return this land to the beauty it once had; the beauty and health which somehow lingers here..."

She again observed her surroundings with awe. The animals exchanged glances, still wary. The great stag spoke.

"The others of your species hunt us," he began. He reminded Nej of the H'nomi Chief, wise and cautious. "My daughter has brought you here, however, and I trust her intuition. Surely she sensed you are different. So tell me...

"How will you renew the forests; the flowers; the rivers; and how will you stop the others of your kind from killing us? As you see, there are very few animals left, and little healthy plant life as well." He addressed the animals gathered as he added, "It is in our best interest to assist you in restoring our land to what it once was."

The animals began to retreat to the pond, to drink and refresh themselves, satisfied with the word of their leader. The stag said "Come, walk with me."

As they casually meandered through the wood near the pond, Nej explained, "I have learned the legend of the Boikk tree..." She thought of her lizard friend then, her storyteller, and wondered where he had gone, and if he was alright. She shook the thought away and tried to focus on her conversation.

"I hope to restore harmony to this land, for all those who want it. I cannot promise that all will go back to the old ways; perhaps some will journey on, finally reach the sea, and travel beyond. But for those who want to live here, and live in peace, I will try."

"I am pleased that one of your kind is finally interested in ending this tiresome war. I suppose you are uncertain how to begin?"

"Yes," Nej answered with some surprise, impressed by how well he understood her struggle. "That is so, I want very much to change things, to do what I can, but I don't know how. I was trying to reach the location of the Boikk tree. Perhaps from there, I will find answers."

The stag nodded his head. "Very good." Then with sufficient pause and pride, he stated, "I have seen the site, of the Boikk tree. And I will direct you in how to find it.

"Simply follow this stream. It is the same stream which once wound around the Boikk tree."

Nej blinked in astonishment.

At last she nodded and managed, "Thank you, very much! I had no idea…"

They moved back toward the pond then. As the buck moved off to join his fellow deer, Nej knelt beside the pond, cupping her hands in the water to draw a drink.

A frog hopped up out of the water and Nej dropped the first handful. Blushing, Nej said, "Pardon me, is this your spot?"

The frog croaked and ignored her query, instead saying, "Heard yer headed fer the great tree."

A little mouse crept out from behind some grasses near the water's edge. "A dangerous task you undertake," she remarked.

"Dangerous?" Nej repeated. "Well I do believe traveling anywhere on our countryside poses significant risk… But if I am successful in my endeavor, we might travel without fear once more," Nej assured.

"Pass through the Golem clan ye may," ventured a second mouse, who came up beside the first. "The Makers," she elaborated.

"Mostly destroyed, they are," the first countered.

"Might be overrun with golems still!" the second carried on. The first rolled her eyes.

Nej chuckled, at last got her drink, then rose.

"Thank you for your advice," she said, then began to follow the stream to the south, and west, as it rambled.

* * *

Nej didn't see the lizard again. She chose to imagine he had returned to and joined the animals of the pond, for, even should she fail her task, there at least he could live in peace and pleasure, and companionship—something she felt he had so far lacked in his life.

A few hours had passed and Nej had left the woodland far behind. Even grasses were growing scarce, and she suspected she was nearing the vast Zenura Desert. That wouldn't be a problem, except that as the land turned dry and barren, so did the stream. And soon she found herself following nothing at all, but the thought that perhaps there was a dip in the ground here, or a trail of stones there, which *might* have been the riverbed, at one time…

In the desert now, it was unclear which way she should be going. Due west or south wouldn't be correct, and she tried to use her intuition to move the right way.

It may not have been the right way to find the tree, but it turned out to be the right path for something else. Each step, or believed misstep, in the journey works toward the ultimate end, even if it doesn't seem to at the time.

She saw a shape rising up in the distance, to the south. She immediately recalled the woodland creatures' warnings, about golems and the Golem clan. But she was not afraid; she needed food, and water, and possibly directional assistance as well. Better to risk entering the sand village.

The village was surrounded by low walls, with sandy mud-daubed houses built up within, the structures supported by wood posts and beams with canvas roof coverings. It looked so still and desolate that Nej wondered at first if it was deserted, but as she neared she heard a voice.

It was singing, softly, half-humming, and as she peeked through a large gap in the wall where the stone had broken and crumbled to the ground, she saw a boy, several years her junior she estimated, sitting beneath a scraggly tree next to one of the sand dwellings. He was working with some scraps of metal and other indistinct articles. She watched and listened.

"…where flowers fly free…" he hummed as he tinkered with this and that and affixed some pieces together, then held his creation aloft in triumph. But a moment later his proud visage turned into a look of concern and he toiled with the object again. He mumbled and hummed as he worked and she made out occasional words, "…stands the Boikk tree…"

Nej smiled.

"Excuse me," she called gently. The boy looked toward the

sound, not quite startled, but clearly surprised to find himself with company.

"Oh...hi," he said simply. "Uh..." rising to his feet and dusting himself off, he added, "Did you need something?"

Nej climbed through the crack in the wall, though she wondered if perhaps the barrier was intended to keep outsiders...out. If so, it certainly wouldn't do a good job in its current condition.

"Well, I have been on a long journey. I hoped I might find food and water here." As she spoke, Nej realized she had nothing to offer in return for such provisions. But she needn't have worried.

"Of course, how thoughtless of me. Come in, please."

The boy led the way into the small hut, which Nej found highly appealing inside. She liked that their village, at least, was stable, and stationary. These homes were not intended to move about. Their way of life seemed superior to her peoples incessant traveling.

There were colorfully woven rugs keeping down the dust on the ground, and thin, vivid-hued diaphanous fabrics interlaced with beaded strings curtaining the many round windows. Built into one wall was a bed, adjacent a small rounded fireplace. Tools; materials of wood, fabric, metal, glass, and more; half-finished creations; artistic decorations; and dozens of books littered the ground, shelves, window ledges, and any other available surfaces.

Whisking a basket of paints and brushes off a low, rough wooden stool, the boy gestured for Nej to have a seat. He next moved some wire contraptions off the stack of stone slabs which served as a table, placing upon it instead a jug of water, a simple clay cup, and a bowl of scones. He pulled up a second stool after brushing the piles of fabrics resting atop it onto the floor.

Nej glanced at him, and they sat in awkward silence for a moment, then he said, "Oh...go ahead," He pushed the food and drink toward her, then got up abruptly, thinking perhaps he shouldn't just sit and watch. He went and grabbed a large, thick book off the bed and brought it back to the table, where he started flipping through it.

As he appeared to be deeply immersed in his reading, Nej selected a pastry and poured some water into the cup. She was ravenous, but tried to partake of the food and drink politely.

He hadn't even asked who she was, and she was grateful that

he would invite her, a stranger, into his home. A very kind young man, she thought.

"My name is Nej," she spoke at last. He looked up immediately from the book, suggesting he hadn't been as interested in it as he had pretended.

"Zuun," he replied.

Nej smiled. "Thank you for the refreshment," she added. "Not everyone would be so generous."

Zuun shrugged. "Was my mother's way," he said in explanation.

"I heard your singing," she continued. His cheeks seemed to redden, though it was hard to tell on account of his deeply tanned skin.

"Heard that ey? Well…"

Nej noted his discomfort and jumped to his rescue.

"Yes it's a song I've only recently learned. It made me wonder if you might know more about the legend?"

He studied her. "Yes…my mother often told the 'legend,' as you say; the story of the Boikk tree?"

Nej nodded.

"My mother taught all the children of our village the story," Zuun smiled slightly as he spoke fondly from memory. "And other stories. She felt that history should be remembered, so we can learn from it."

Nej smiled. "She sounds very wise." Nej then frowned, in thought.

"In fact, my people are supposed to be wise—they study magic and healing, always trying to improve their knowledge. But they never speak of the legend, or of the past. Ancient history is irrelevant to them."

Zuun considered this. "My people too," he agreed, "Are supposed to be great thinkers; great builders. But most don't care to remember what happened before. The most they remember is that golems have killed many of us, and so now we build better golems to protect ourselves!"

He chuckled, and it made Nej laugh too.

"And does that work?"

Zuun gave a sly grin and stood. "Come," he said, and passed through a bead-draped doorway beside the fireplace. Nej stood and followed.

Through the back door, and a short hallway, they emerged

under a large canopy on the east side of the house. And there stood…

"A golem!" Nej gasped.

Zuun grinned. "My best friend," he said proudly.

Nej stepped closer to the golem. It was not so large as the ones she had fought. This one seemed much more…loved. Its parts were haphazard, but it looked like an individual had painstakingly connected all the wires and gears, crystals and bolts, with great care. Not perfectly done, but lovingly done. She reached out and touched the golem's metal arm; it moved, and she jerked back.

The golem turned its head and stared at her with mismatched eyes, one a glowing light, the other twisting gears. "A pleasure," the golem stated, in monotone staccato. Nej smiled and her eyes twinkled with fascination.

"He is incredible," she said to Zuun. Then, "You are incredible," she added, with a nod to the golem.

Turning to Zuun she asked, "How did you do this? And how can you be certain he will not turn on you, as the others did?"

"Well…just because one person is bad, doesn't mean they all are."

Nej was momentarily speechless. His logic was much as hers would typically be, and she felt ashamed that she hadn't drawn the same conclusion herself.

"You're quite right. I wouldn't judge an individual by his or her species, or tribe. We don't choose our birth, or creation. Actions must determine one's character.

"But you understand my concern," she tried to explain. "I suppose the true question would be, what made the golems turn on your people in the first place?"

Zuun nodded, and motioned, and the two of them took a seat on a low wood bench resting against the warm sandy wall.

He took a deep breath, exhaling slowly, gazing at the darkening sky, the clouds turning pink and orange as the sun began to fall behind the mountains far in the west.

"My golem is named Jett," Zuun began at last. He glanced at Nej. "He's my best friend. That is why he won't turn on me, and, in a way, why the other golems did."

Nej nodded, trying to understand.

"Long ago, the first Zenurans to build golems, built many: not just one person building a friend, but many building an army. An army to do all their bidding and more. To build homes and grow food, to defend against enemies; to work and slave for them, to die for them. And because they were only machines, they needn't receive anything in return for their service. Not a kind word or gesture, not even thanks.

"And so, these intelligent creatures, even if they were more machine than organic—they were, and are, still *alive*. And they began to see the disparity in their treatment. And...they realized they were much stronger than their creators." This last statement hung chillingly, ominously in the air, before Zuun continued.

"It is said that it was a water golem who first rebelled. Water golems are usually calm and peaceful, but their thoughts run deep. It is said that one day, one water golem decided he wanted to live his own life, by his own rules. Not slave for the Zenura, bringing them water, creating rivers and irrigation for their crops. He wanted to be free. And so he lashed out. He scattered water everywhere, and he yelled that he would not be prisoner to his makers will any longer.

"Well the Zenura said he was broken, that he needed repairs. They tried to subdue him. But apparently he wasn't the only one who felt...unjustly subjugated. One after another, more golems turned on the Zenurans. The Zenurans fought back. Many Zenurans died."

"I'm sorry," Nej said consolingly.

Zuun gave a little smile. "Nah, this is ancient history! Admittedly the Zenuran numbers were reduced, perhaps much sooner and faster than any other tribes..." he chuckled.

"But I think now, we're closer to even, after centuries of war amongst the others—or so I've heard."

"Yes, there is much fighting between the other clans," Nej affirmed, "At least, the Tayuuk, the Entari, and my own people, the H'nomi."

Zuun smiled. "You would be with the peaceful ones."

Nej sighed. "Perhaps we are peaceful, but we weren't when we aided in the destruction of the tree."

"True. When desperate for change, and influenced by others, people may act out of character."

"Or maybe, show their true character."

Zuun chuckled.

"Anyway," Zuun returned to his story, "that was long ago. The Zenurans fled deeper into the desert, while the golems split in all directions, mostly staying with their own kind. Earth to the mountains, water to the rivers, air were happy in the desert or open grasslands. After a few nights in the desert, the Zenurans returned here, to our village, and rebuilt. Since then there have been other golem attacks..."

"Why do the golems come back? Do they actively seek you out?"

Zuun shook his head.

"Not sure. Still spiteful?" he hazarded to guess. "Would have to ask them, though one can speculate.

"But with my own golem," Zuun added, more lightheartedly, "I hope to convince both Zenura and golemkind that we can live peacefully together. We just need to show them the respect they deserve."

"I'm sure you will, Zuun," Nej agreed.

As he looked at her, Nej was impressed by the vivid, deep blue of his eyes, and the contrast of his very pale hair as a few strands fell in front of his face. Truly the harsh desert sun was to blame for the dark and lightness of his skin and hair, respectively.

"I appreciate how you want to bring peace to your people, Zuun," Nej said. "I too want peace, but on an even larger scale."

"How so?"

"That legend, you know the part, where the tree was destroyed? And there was something inside?"

Zuun's brow furrowed. "What of it."

"Well, each of the leaders has a piece of it—a piece of that thing, from the tree. And one of the leaders said, I could make it whole again. He suggested that maybe, somehow, doing that could end all this fighting amongst our clans."

Zuun whistled.

"You don't say. Why didn't anyone think of that before?"

"I don't think many actually want peace, or thought it was possible. As I mentioned, I had never heard of the legend before. My people don't tell it."

"You're right at that. People don't have time for old stories, true or not. Too much work every day just trying to survive. I only know it because my mother used to tell it to all us village children, when I was little, when she'd be watching us. But most probably thought it was just a story, nothing more."

"But not you?"

He grinned. "I had my mother around a lot more than

68

they did. I heard her stories more often. And I had time to ask questions."

Nej suddenly looked sad, and said softly, guessing she needn't even ask, "Where is she?"

Zuun smiled slightly, then glanced up to the sky, at the stars now glistening above them.

"You know, my mother and I, we wanted to live together forever. We wanted to experience this world for centuries, watching it change and grow, enjoying its beauty. But during the golem attacks, when I was a child, I was afraid something would happen to ruin our dream.

"So my mother told me—and I didn't really believe it mind, but it was a reassuring thought—she said, if she ever had to leave, she'd be reborn on our lands, and that she'd find me again."

He chuckled and looked away.

"I know it sounds crazy and sentimental. But she said she loved me so much she'd come back. She said she would always be there for me. She said, she knew we both wanted to live forever, but that in a way, in my memory, she would.

"She said that someday, even though she might not remember me, and I might not recognize her, that we'd find each other and spend our lives together—share in each others lives again. That it's in the soul, and that when you meet a person whose soul touches yours, you just know it."

He chuckled again, then glanced at her, and his face grew serious. "You remind me of her. Maybe she wasn't just saying it."

Nej smiled politely.

"Besides, if anyone could make *that* happen, it'd be her. She was passionate and adamant…"

"I see those qualities in you, too. You're determined to change the world for the better.

"Can you help me, Zuun. I need to get to the tree, to learn what I can do: how to get these fragments, and what to do with them once I have them."

Zuun blinked, coming out of his memories. "Oh…yeah! Yeah, sure, happy to, Nej…"

"Do you know the way? A…" Nej hesitated. Did this boy believe animals could speak? "I," she corrected, "was told that I should simply follow the river, to the tree, but the river has dried up."

Zuun nodded. "Sure has. Without the golems; without the

tree..." He shook his head.

"But yeah, I know the way."

"You do! Well then please, direct me, or you may accompany me if you desire, though I don't wish to inconvenience you."

"No, I'd love to go along, sounds like a great adventure!" He got to his feet.

"My mother and I used to walk far beyond the village, to the mountains even." Zuun gestured and paced as he talked. "I think the path you want is further south. And with Jett we should have no trouble crossing the mountain range."

* * *

They spent the night in Zuun's hut, then at daybreak Nej awoke to the sounds of Zuun bustling in and out and all around, gathering food and water and various trinkets, tossing this and that into bags, strapping an assortment of daggers and other articles to his belt.

She sat up and stretched. "You're so efficient," she complimented, as she watched him race to and fro.

He stopped and smiled. "Well we want an early start right? Long walk ahead of us."

"Yes, of course," she stood. "And you've already gathered everything we might need. And then some."

"Thought about it over the night," he admitted.

"I'm glad you're looking forward to our trip. I'm really grateful for all your help."

"Think nothing of it," he waved a hand dismissively. "What am I here. Nothing. But this is a chance to do something—something big.

"Well...you ready? Want a bite before we go?" he added.

She shook her head. "Just a little water maybe, and I'm ready."

"I've already spoken to Jett too," Zuun rambled as he found the water jug and brought it to Nej. "He's eager to travel, maybe even see some of his own kind." Zuun grinned.

As they stepped out into the clear, cool morning, Nej shivered and wished the sun would rise a little faster.

"Is it always this cold in the desert?"

"Only at night," Zuun assured. "Don't worry, before we reach the mountains, we'll be wishing for some shade."

They stepped around to the back of Zuun's hut to collect Jett, who, with great clicks and clangs and whirring and venting of steam, straightened up and began stepping forward. They exited through the broken section of wall and began moving opposite the rising sun.

"We'll go mostly south," Zuun commented. "For one, I'm not sure exactly how far south we have to go, and for two, if you say Tayuuk and Entari and even your people are up north, well, we don't need to run into them just now."

Nej nodded. "Too far south is better than too far north," she agreed.

"Think I know a plateau that spans the range," Zuun gestured, "Be easier to pass through by that, than to climb even higher."

"Sure."

They trudged onward; Zuun asked about Nej's people, and the other clans she had met. She explained how her people and the Entari had been traveling for centuries, and still had gotten nowhere. How they continually battled any time their paths crossed, and how their numbers had been greatly reduced.

He asked how she learned of the legend, and she said evasively, "It's a rather long story..."

"We've got a rather long walk," Zuun grinned. So Nej elaborated on her capture by the Entari, the difficult return to her own people, the Tayuuk spell, the lizard...

"Woa, what? You can talk to animals too?"

Nej blushed and laughed nervously. "I don't know, I guess I can."

She concluded that the Tayuuk leader had hinted about the legend, and the lizard had filled her in on the rest. Her tale finished, Nej in turn asked Zuun more about golems, and he spoke at length about the types of golems, his golem, building golems... she had clearly found his passion, and Nej was content to listen silently.

Zuun described parts of his own golem and how they were brought to life. To Nej, Jett was fascinating. Nej had never seen a functioning golem close up without it attacking her.

"It's amazing that you alone have built your very own golem— and that unlike the rest, he is peaceful."

"We respect each other," Zuun said. "I think," he glanced at the golem.

"Of course I am pleased with Zuun, my creator," Jett spoke up. "He has given me no cause to dislike."

"Except maybe when I talk too much," Zuun suggested.

"Ha - ha. Zuun, talk much," affirmed Jett.

Their southwestern path brought them to the eastern edge of the mountains by mid-morning. With Jett's assistance they scaled the rocky mountainside quickly, and soon found themselves on a bluff overlooking the desert on one side, and on the other, the great plains.

They paused to eat the provisions Zuun had brought along, both silently observing the view of the desert, even Zuun's village, barely a speck in the distance. Jett milled about, monitoring; guarding.

When they had eaten their fill and had sufficient rest, they pressed on to the far west side of the plateau. Here they were greeted by an expansive view of the once fertile valley. Trees still lined the mountain face, but the green plant life faded away into dry dirt at the base. Even worse were the deep crevices where the land seemed to be splitting apart. Some gorges appeared extremely deep. The cracks were radiating from a point off to the west. Nej sensed that point was likely the place they were seeking.

"Well..." Zuun said uncertainly.

"Yes. We must continue, it must be there." Nej insisted. Zuun glanced at Jett with a shrug, then began the descent into the barren valley.

Dried, brown grasses littered the ground here and there; an occasional grey, dead tree creaked and swayed in the hot breeze which brushed over them. The ground was falling apart beneath their feet. Parts were soft and crumbling, and great gaps cut deep into the earth.

The land sloped gently downward, until it dropped abruptly at the lip of a wide but shallow crater, the curving border of which appeared to be the depleted bed of the ancient river oxbow. The long, deep cracks extended from and widened as they approached the center of the crater, and the mountain behind them cast a distinct shadow over that central point.

"This is it," Nej looked all around her, taking in the surroundings as a whole. "The cracks...they're where the trees roots rested, now rotting away..."

They climbed down into the crater, but the crevices impaired their movement, and occasionally they had to jump aside as large sections of ground gave way beneath their feet. The ground was thickly coated by a charred mixture of loose soil, ash, wood, and rock.

As they neared the center, more and larger fragments of wood lay strewn about, though it seemed many pieces must have tumbled into the depths of the gaping rifts, for there was not enough debris to account for an entire tree of the Boikk's magnitude.

"I don't think we can get close enough," Zuun said, sidestepping as his feet sank into the deteriorating earth.

"This place is crazy!" he added. "How can we ever repair it?"

Nej slowly shook her head.

CHAPTER 7
The Boikk Tree

"I really don't see how we can get to the center," Zuun said dejectedly. Nej nodded. "Let's see what we can learn from here."

They began picking through the debris.

"This is where the end of our land begins," Nej remarked.

"I'd say so," Zuun agreed. "The Boikk tree was the source of life for our little world. As the tree decays, so does the land around."

"Look how deep these rifts go! If this continues, our continent will one day be nothing but a giant hole!"

Zuun repeatedly picked up, examined, and dropped pieces of wood and chunks of rock.

"What about beyond?" he inquired. "Is there a beyond? You say your people were going to the sea. The Entari, to the sea. Everyone talks about the sea, but no one ever gets there. Something must be there, right?"

Before Nej could respond, Zuun suddenly tilted his head, staring down at something on the ground. Nej approached and they both knelt, looking at a piece of wood, grey and worn. But something was drawn and etched into the bark.

"A flower?" Zuun guessed. Nej began to smile.

"A flying flower?" she asked hopefully, then added, "They drew on the tree? There were…images on it?" She sighed. "I would love to have seen it. To see these…" She brushed her fingers lightly over the carving on the wood, hoping it wouldn't fall apart. Her brow furrowed.

"How lucky that this one piece is still intact,"

Zuun shrugged, rising. "But where is the rest of it? So little is here, for such an enormous tree. There's just tiny bits of wood."

They scanned their surroundings. Zuun mused aloud, "You know, they say—the legend says, that those rebels cut down the tree, then found something in the stump. But, maybe they didn't just slice through the trunk, clean and simple. I'd say they demolished it."

Nej felt her heart sink further as she realized that must be true. They burned it and smashed it and tore it down until it wasn't recognizable. Wood was scattered all about and stomped to dirt, though a few larger bits remained.

"Such violence. No wonder..." She trailed off and Zuun glanced at her.

"No wonder what?"

"No wonder things have been so bad since. A revolution spawned of hate will only spread more hate. Our people kill one another thoughtlessly, and feel no remorse in the pain they cause. Even our environment is suffering from the senseless violence. And the tree has given up on us all—it no longer tries to help, because we don't deserve its help."

"I guess so, but it was just a tree, what could it know? It doesn't have a choice; it's just gone. It can't give or take anything now. But I agree, the manic destruction our ancestors enacted continues to fuel our war today."

Nej nodded absently. "Yes...but, what if it isn't *just a tree*," she pondered. "And what if it isn't *completely* gone. I feel like something is here."

Zuun frowned. "Not much here."

"An aura perhaps," she continued, reaching a hand out, "as if part of the tree has been holding on—in case someone came back."

Closing her eyes, Nej tried to feel the presence more fully. She tried to focus on the energy around her and draw it more strongly into existence. She heard Zuun mutter something unintelligible, but she kept her thoughts on the tree. She didn't notice that a soft glow was overtaking her, and that the breeze was picking up.

Nej felt the presence close by, in the air all around, and she tried to convey a message, *I'm sorry for what they did. Please teach me how to bring you back*. There was a nerve-wracking pause, and Nej began to believe it was just her imagination, that nothing was there at all. And then, like a whisper of wind, a voice seemed to float across the air:

"Fill the Void,
Replenish the River,
Plant a new Seed,
To grow here Forever."

And with a gust of wind the tree's voice disappeared. Nej opened her eyes and inhaled deeply. She turned to Zuun, who looked wide-eyed and thoughtful.

"You heard?"

He nodded, clearly a believer now, then looked toward his golem.

"Replenish the the river," he mused, "Golems—water golems—could fill up that river for you."

Nej raised an eyebrow. "They can do that? I never knew. That is impressive, but who will convince them to do it for us? You?"

Zuun chuckled. "Water golems...are some of the most volatile. They don't like us very much. But Jett, he might be able to coax them." He turned to the golem.

"What do you say?"

Jett replied thoughtfully, "Where do we fit? If tree returns, what happens to golems?"

Zuun squinted his eyes.

"Whaddya mean?" he asked in annoyance. Nej cleared her throat, and Zuun gazed upward and took a deep breath, trying to quell his impatience before correcting his reply.

"I don't know, Jett, but I really don't think you'd just disappear, do you? And we certainly aren't going to get rid of you. You might not have been here the *first* time, but then, we don't want to have a repeat of the *first* time, do we. It'd be nice to keep some of our...better mistakes, around, as a reminder of why not to make the same bad mistakes again."

Nej stepped nearer, adding gently, "Jett, of course the golems would be treated with the same respect and kindness as any other race or clan. I have no desire to ostracize any, and returning to peace, means peace for all."

Jett's gears whirred and he inclined his head toward Nej, approving her words.

"Then, with the help of the golems, we would be able to bring fresh water—"

"And dirt," interjected Zuun, kicking at the ground. "Earth golems," he clarified.

Nej nodded. "And maybe some of my clan's mages would be able to assist."

"But we still have to talk to them–all of them. The golems, the clans. We need the 'seed,' which could be those fragments I really don't want to go find."

"But it can be done!" Nej said enthusiastically. "Don't you see. Just knowing we can do it makes it worth trying! Even if it takes—"

"Is it really worth it?"

She frowned, hurt by Zuun's sudden negativity. "Well what else should we be doing? What else is there to do? Continue running from hunters and warriors? Fight golems? Play with magic and machines? Why not make a difference in our world? Instead of just bettering ourselves, better our people as a whole! Save the animals and plants and people all at once. Then we can all work together instead of separately, and work toward common goals for good, not fighting all the time.

"It's so silly!" Nej continued, "The fights! They're fights over nothing at all! Fighting just to fight, just to hunt. I won't be a part of it anymore. The world as it is isn't worth living in. But we can change it. We can make it better!"

"How do we know it will be better? They hated it enough before to destroy the tree. Savagely!" Zuun gestured at the ruins around them. "How much they must have hated it to do this much damage! And we want to set it all back the way it was? I'm not so sure that's a good idea."

Nej stared aghast. Zuun had been so supportive until now. She hoped he was arguing simply to offer an alternate perspective. She had contemplated similar possibilities when she first heard the legend—that perhaps no one else wanted peace, and perhaps it wouldn't last, just as before. Thinking of the legend reminded her of her lizard friend. She wished she had his advice. Not that he had pushed his opinions, but he gave suggestions which lead her to a different way of thinking. She recalled when she had planned to warn the Entari, but his words had persuaded her to instead address the Tayuuk.

With an exasperated sigh she sunk to the ground, frustrated

at coming so far, only to be unsure yet again of how to proceed. But what was there, other than this? Go back to one clan or another? Live out her days with Zuun, learning about golems and magic or traveling the country? Was that life worth it? Not changing a thing, just existing, in this world their ancestors had forged? Was Zuun really afraid to bring back the tree? Not *everyone* had wanted it destroyed after all. In fact, only a handful had wished it, and acted on that desire.

"Zuun," Nej spoke resolutely, "Just as some of our ancestors desperately wanted change long ago, I want it again. Maybe they were wrong, and I might be too. But I don't think I'm the only one. And I think it's time to see if anyone else feels the way I do." She stood up, dusting herself off, and looked around, deciding which way she should go.

"Fair enough," Zuun said. "We've gone this far, why not see how many would want to bring back the tree.

"Meanwhile," he turned to the golem. "Will you find the golems, and try to take care of the earth and water problems? We could use your help getting us to the other clans, but I think you're best suited to persuade the golems to join us."

The golem agreed, "I will go."

"And let us meet back here after..." Nej thought a moment, "After five nights pass. On the dawning of the fifth day."

Zuun whistled. "You don't waste time."

"I have a feeling this tree is in a bad state and we don't have much longer before our task may be futile."

Zuun nodded. "As quickly as we can then."

With no further ado the golem turned and headed back the way they came. Zuun seemed agitated, almost distraught as he watched his golem leaving. They had always been together; Jett's companionship had helped keep Zuun going after the loss of his mother, with whom he had been exceedingly close. Nej sensed this and felt such discomfort she said, "Why don't you go with him, Zuun? Help him locate and befriend the golems, and perhaps find the fragment from your tribe as well?"

He turned and smiled at her. "And leave you to find all the rest? Four clans, spread out across the entire continent?"

"But three I already know well, and I have a good idea of their whereabouts. I will try the Koi'Tan first, to the south, because I've never encountered them before and so it seems the most difficult."

"I should go with you. It will be dangerous in the jungle."

"You haven't seen me fight," she said confidently. "I believe I can handle anything.

"If only we had a way to keep in touch, though. This continent is so vast, we'll have no idea where the other is, and if one does get into trouble…"

"We'd likely never find each other. True enough," Zuun agreed. "I may have a solution.

"My people are inventors as you know. I made this," he rummaged in his floppy canvas bag until he withdrew a tiny device, not much more than a switch with a couple little lights on it.

"It isn't much, but it communicates with my golem. Push the switch if you're in trouble; the red light will turn on so you'll know he's coming. The blue light will glow if he needs help; when you face the array, that's this silver area, toward him, the light will be brightest, so you know you're going the right direction."

He handed the object to her, and she gave him a hug, which he returned.

"Thank you," she said.

"Good luck," he smiled, then ran off after his golem, whose large form was plainly visible lumbering in the distance.

CHAPTER 8
The Koi'Tan

With a deep sigh, Nej tore her gaze away from the figures disappearing to the east, and turned south to begin her journey, solo once more, into the Koi'Tan jungle.

She could already see the dark green treetops looming far beyond the grassy plains. Nej moved quickly across the burning crater of crumbling earth and into the tall grasses. There was no shade here, not until the jungle, which grew suddenly, with no transition or warning, in the deep valley comprising the southern tip—the lowest region of the continent. Her mouth felt dry and her skin was burning from the unfiltered sunlight, hot breeze, and her fast pace. And yet the jungle was near now, and the promise of shade and water urged her onward, so that it was barely midday when she stumbled to the edge of the cliff at the outskirts of the great ravine.

The sun was high and bright, and Nej was exceedingly grateful for the relief of the jungle canopy. However, after a few moments of climbing across enormous vine-covered branches in the sweltering combination of humidity and heat, Nej wondered if it wouldn't be more pleasant out in the open air again. Furthermore, she required constant vigilance for danger here; she had heard tales of the hostile jungle plants and creatures, armed with poisons, sharp fangs, claws, and thorns.

Nej crawled along a wide branch until she hit a giant, impassable trunk; looking for a viable path, she saw a sturdy limb slightly below her and grabbed some hanging vines to lower herself down to it. As she gave her full weight to the vines, something snapped, and she gave a shout as she fell hard onto the branch below, knocking the wind out of herself, leaving her gasping for breath. A gentle sound, of brushing leaves or fabric, rippled to the left of her, and she slowly shifted her eyes then head toward the source of the sound. She saw a large flower, as tall as she was, unwinding its expansive petals. As she began to push herself up, she saw a couple more, nestled against a heavily plant-and-vine-embellished tree trunk, opening as well.

Nej made an uncertain sound, unable to contain the bad feeling engendered by these beautiful, fearfully large blossoms. And in a split second, they fired upon her!

Nearly glowing yellow-green fluid spit from their stamen, hissing and steaming wherever it landed. Nej ducked and slid, gripping the branch she was on so just her arms held her aloft, her feet dangling over what looked to be a very long drop. Some of the goo struck her arm in a streak and she cried out and tried to brush it off against the tree. It burned and left a mark where it had touched her skin. The flowers released another round of spray and Nej was forced to let go.

Her fall was interrupted by several small branches, none of which she was able to catch hold of, and as she fell lower, vines and tree limbs broke under her weight until she finally hit earth. She laid motionless for a moment, staring upward, collecting herself after the episode. It was almost peaceful, watching the gentle rain of leaves dance to the ground, the aftermath of her intrusion. In her silence, she heard trickling of water nearby, and buzzing of insects here and there, as well as cracks of twigs and underbrush as creatures, she supposed, moved about across the jungle floor. *Best to keep moving*, Nej half-muttered to herself. Sore and bruised, but perhaps unbroken, Nej groaned as she tried to sit up. And she froze mid-attempt, as she saw glowing eyes before her, slinking through the foliage.

"Oh no…" she breathed. She was exhausted, and her entire body ached, but she struggled to think of a plan, a way to save herself from this new foe. She didn't know what it was called, it almost reminded her of Tayuuk, but on four legs, and more feline in appearance. But instead of soft fur it had a scaly body, as if part reptilian. She saw gleaming spines on its tail which it suddenly whipped towards her. She rolled left, into some leaves, and kept rolling until she splashed into a shallow brook. She gasped at the coldness of the water. There was a crashing in the brush from whence she'd came and the croco-cat burst through the same path she'd taken. But instead of striking at her where she lay in the water, the creature stared across at another new beast who had been taking a drink before Nej disturbed it.

Nej lay still with the water rushing over and around her. The cat-beast growled and took a few steps backward, baring its teeth and crouching as if to pounce. The new creature stood on two hind legs, also had scaled skin, but with a vividly-colored, stripey pattern, as opposed to the firsts' solid dark hue. The second bared its long teeth, some of which were always exposed, and gave a sharp battle cry; then the cat-beast sprang at him.

While the two creatures wrestled, Nej crawled further south through the brook. When she reached a fall, she scrambled over the edge and hastened down the slippery, moss-coated rocks there. Despite her caution, she mistrusted a foothold and splashed into the small pool of water below. She swam to the bank and painfully dragged herself ashore, the sounds of the fight still audible on the ridge overhead. But a new danger presented itself yet again: pointy spears with glossy, vile green slime painted on their tips were thrust into her face, and she dared not move.

Letting her eyes alone examine the humanoids, she discovered they were all handsome figures, and looking like perfectly natural men, aside from perhaps, being somewhat tall and fairly well-built. Their muscles rippled distinctly across their sun-darkened skin. She heard gentle steps of one as he neared, from her side where she could not see. Some spears were lifted to allow him to approach. She felt him stop beside her, and wondered if it would be safe to move now.

"She is not Koi'Tan," a deep voice spoke, from just above her.

"Take her to the Queen," it added. In a rush all the spears were whisked aside and hands grabbed her roughly, lifting her to her feet. She felt light headed from the abrupt change in position and from the numerous falls she had endured, and was relieved for the support, callous as it was. They half dragged her through the thick jungle, until at last they reached a sort of clearing, and an array of vine-enveloped rock structures formed their village.

Nej hadn't made any effort to speak; her captors had given no indication they desired her to. And she felt it best to follow their lead, in their territory. At least she felt safer amongst reasoning individuals than amongst the primal killers at wild in the jungle.

She was lead down to their village and escorted through a maze of narrow pathways and tunnels until they reached an underground chamber, delightfully cool: a great cave with water running through, falling from the walls at the back of the cave and filling the enclave as a dark blue pool. This water separated the cave entry from a raised stone platform on which rested a flower-wreathed throne. Vines, ferns, succulent green plants, and vibrant flowers filled the walls of the cave, and a sparkling shaft of sunlight filtered in through a wide crack near the ceiling, shining down upon the throne.

More guards stood about the cave, and on the throne posed an enchanting young woman, looking as exotic, beautiful, and dangerous as the poisonous flowers Nej had encountered. The woman's golden eyes flashed as they darted toward Nej, who took note of her immaculate, caramel-colored skin and sleek black hair smoothed into a high pony tail, which extended to the middle of her back. She wore all manner of gold embellishments; earrings, bracelets, necklaces, diadems. Her clothing was loose and revealing, though fine and delicate in material and design.

"My Queen," the deep-voiced captor stepped forward and bowed his head. "We found this trespasser on the north ridge. Perhaps another rebel posing as a lost traveler."

The Queen looked disdainfully upon Nej. Nej suspected she looked a mess. Even her clothes hadn't fully dried, despite the midday heat, with the humidity of the jungle. She knew she was covered in bruises, scratches, gashes, burns, and dirt. Perhaps more. Two guards still supported her arms, and she found, though their grasp was uncomfortably harsh, she was grateful for the assistance as she felt exceedingly weak and desperately needed a moments rest. Her head spun and she wondered if she hadn't hit it too hard on one of her many recent falls.

She suddenly remembered she could heal her injuries, if only she would have a chance.

"A spy of Hervana," the Queen spoke, dismissively, with a thick, rich accent. Her words were clear and concise; artfully chosen, and when she spoke everyone paid attention.

Nej opened her mouth to speak but the Queen shot her such a glare that she closed it again with a sigh and lowered her eyes in defeat. But this gesture softened the Queen. She rose, and gestured to the guards, who released Nej. The motion was so sudden, and Nej so weak, she almost crumpled to the ground, but managed to lower herself gently enough to her hands and knees, where she tried to collect herself and prepare for what was to come.

The Queen approached her, stepping across a row of stones extruding from the water. Her diaphanous, violet skirt trailed behind her and barely brushed the pool. She too crouched down, examining Nej.

"Have you another story?"

Nej looked up at her hopefully, not wanting to miss an opportunity to set the record straight.

"Yes," she whispered, "Yes I have, Your Highness. May I share it?"

The Queen pursed her lips in a tight smile and stood. "Proceed," she permitted, with a wave of her hand as she walked slowly away from Nej.

With a deep breath, Nej began, "I am new to your jungle. I have sought you out, because I require your aid. My name is Nej, and I am from the H'nomi clan—"

Turning sharply back, the Queen said with a laugh, "You expect me to believe you made it through the northern ridge of the jungle alive as a foreigner?"

Nej blinked. "Is that…unusual?"

The Queen laughed again. Nej stifled an involuntary smile; the laughter was pleasant, but she could see the Queen was not yet convinced.

"I am a scout, M'lady…"

"Ahh yes, verily you are, but for which clan?"

Before Nej could reply, the Queen continued, "And if you are a scout, you did a poor job of eluding my sentinels."

Nej sighed. "Sometimes discussion can be more fruitful than subterfuge." She explained, "I need your help, M'lady. I could not, and had no desire to hide forever, as I needed to find and speak with you alone."

Narrowing her eyes, the Queen replied skeptically, "How would a foreigner know of me? It is far more likely you are a servant of my enemy, sent to infiltrate and deceive me, as countless have attempted before."

"Please, I am not here to deceive you—"

"Ahh," the Queen interrupted. "enough talk. Prove your loyalty and you will have my trust and my aid, as you claim to desire. Fail and you shall lose your life."

Nej heard some murmurs and shuffling of the guards in the room at this ultimatum.

"Vai'shun," the Queen addressed the deep-voiced man, clearly a servant of high rank, "Take Ruvar and...*Nej*, to the outpost on the eastern hillside. Observe for Separatists over the night and return at dawn if no threat is perceived."

Vai'shun bowed his head to the Queen, then turned and strode past Nej, who rose unsteadily to her feet. Another guard from the original party tapped her shoulder, and ceremoniously removed his bow and quiver, holding them out to Nej.

"Thank you," she said softly as she accepted the offer. He smiled.

"I'm Ruvar. You'll need something to protect you out there." Nej blushed at his kindness, and at everyone seeing the exchange. However, her face fell as she caught sight of Vai'shun, who had paused at the cave entrance and was staring at her with a venomous expression. With a scowl he strode away, and Nej and Ruvar raced to catch up.

Vai'shun walked quickly through the tunnels, then the village, and into the eastern grasslands. At the outskirts of the village spanned a broad clearing, much of which was turned into farmland, riddled with garden plants bearing colorful edibles, terminating at a ridge to the east, where the land fell away into the river. Nej thought how fortunate the Koi'Tan were, to live in the only remaining region that was lush and verdant, with ample water. However, the jungle's dangers were no trifle.

Although Vai'shun seemed averse to her presence, the second soldier was attentive, speaking to her at length as they walked to their destination.

"So you really have never entered the jungle before?"

Nej smiled. "No, I have not before this day."

He whistled softly, admiration showing on his face. "Amazing you weren't killed!"

Vai'shun spoke up harshly, "That's because we found her. If we'd left her any longer she would have been."

Ruvar rolled his eyes, and Vai'shun quickened his pace, putting more distance between himself and the pair.

Ruvar came nearer Nej and said more quietly, "Then you don't really know what we're doing."

Nej looked at him curiously, then haltingly admitted, "I suppose I don't understand fully."

"Well," he began, his voice tinged with excitement, "Me, Vai'shun, and all our village, we're Loyalists, loyal to the Queen, once Niahla, now Tiore." He abruptly glanced ahead at Vai'shun, who apparently hadn't overheard. Nej suspected Vai'shun might not approve of Ruvar revealing so much information to her.

He looked back at Nej, his eyes meeting hers in his sincerity. "But not all the Koi'Tan are Loyalists. We've been fighting for decades, with the Separatists: the Koi'Tan rebels who committed treason against our Queen Niahla." Ruvar rushed on enthusiastically, "One of her handmaidens, Hervana, now the rebel leader, poisoned Niahla! Then nearly half the Koi'Tan joined Hervana when Niahla died—"

"Ruvar!" They had reached the eastern watchtower, and Vai'shun was glaring at them.

"Prepare the tower for our overnight stay."

He glanced haughtily at Nej. "You. Cross the river. Search the treeline for signs of Separatists."

Nej gave a nod and started past him, when he added in a hiss, "This is your last chance to escape. I'm being more than generous."

She looked back at him, saddened by his avid dislike for her, then removed the bow and quiver from her shoulder and set them down beside the tower. "I cannot leave, for my task here is not yet complete," she stated calmly. "But I do not require these. I do not know the difference between a Loyalist and Separatist, nor do I wish to harm either. Your fight is not mine; I have come for something else." Ruefully shaking her head, she moved down the short, rocky cliff toward the water's edge.

He watched after her for a bit, then, after a calculating glance at the weapon she had left behind, collected the bow and arrows and passed pointedly through the dark, tattered curtain that formed the door into the tower.

Nej reached the bank and easily crossed the placid, shallow water. The eastern shore was overgrown with ferns, grasses, and flowers, and the large jungle trees grew only steps from the water's edge, their long branches hanging down and shading the river. Nej had no desire to enter into the foliage, now fully aware of what awaited within. Staying along the muddy bank, she trained her eyes into the deeply shaded forest, looking for any signs of movement.

Suddenly there was a shout from the tower. Nej looked back in alarm, immediately wading back across the river, wondering what could have happened in so short a time.

She scrambled up the rocks, but slowed and was on her guard as she circumnavigated the tower. She felt a mixture of urgency and caution, and thought it best to assess the situation from outside first. Walking straight into an unfamiliar, enclosed space with only one exit might be unwise, especially when there was now the threat of danger. Had some enemy been hiding inside before they arrived? Nej hoped the guards were alright. She found a rope-and-vine ladder on the northern face of the tower, the side opposite the doorway, partially obscured by weeds and bushes growing up around the tower's base. Nej opted to take this entrance inside.

The ladder went to the top of the tower, where Nej climbed over a low stone wall onto an open overlook. A gap in the floor revealed another rope ladder leading inside. Nej crouched on the wood boards and stared down into the darkness, but saw nothing. With a deep breath, she decided to risk it. She slid into the gap, swinging gingerly down the rope rungs until she landed softly on the lower level.

She was in what looked like a storage room, and out the single open doorway was a ramp leading down toward the main floor, where the guards had entered. She crept cautiously down the ramp, annoyed by the torch glowing on the wall in front of her, making too clear her presence.

To the left at the end of the ramp was another small room, with hammocks lining the walls and chests of gear and supplies lying open on the ground. Some weapons hung near the doorway. A glance inside revealed no signs of life.

Nej felt her anxiety growing as she turned around, to the right path. Whatever she sought, or had heard, must be found there, in the main room at the tower's entrance. Peeking around the wood-framed entryway, she saw a fire glowing in one corner of the room; a table and chairs against the wall near her; a few supply chests and shelves, and, near the window…

"Ruvar!" she gasped, and rushed to him, forgetting all concern for her own safety. He was slumped against the stone wall, an arrow protruding from his back. Tears stung in her eyes as she tried to shift him, to see if he was still alive. Suddenly she sensed something behind her. She froze, then slowly began to turn around when a heavy blow struck the back of her head and the world went dark.

* * *

Nej woke up bruised, bloody, and in chains. She felt pain everywhere. Knowing she was now in real trouble, she tried to think what she could do. Her thoughts flashed to Zuun and that device—if she could contact Zuun! But looking down, she saw her clothes were in tatters and her dagger and hip satchel were missing.

Seeing her awake, a guard approached and made as if to strike her; she jerked her head away and he chuckled.

"Thought you could pull one over on us did you," he said coldly.

"I don't know what you mean," she implored. "I did nothing—"

He moved again as if to strike and she fell silent, hanging her head.

"Please may I speak to your Queen," she asked in a whisper.

"Got a plan to murder her too?" the guard mocked. With a grunt he moved away from her.

Nej's eyebrows furrowed. What could he mean? What had happened...

She realized she wouldn't get any more information out of the guard. His mind seemed set against her. Keeping her head lowered, she glanced around her prison. Naturally, it was dark, aside from a tiny hole, a sort of natural oculus near the top of the cave behind her. The dim reddish light filtering through the gap spoke of sunset and foretold of dusk.

But the lingering crimson glow was still enough to see by. She supposed a prisoner wasn't worthy of a torch light. And perhaps the guard went upstairs at nightfall. He must have been stationed here just for her, as no other prisoners were present, as far as she could tell.

It was clear this was a cave that had been found, not created. There were chains fixed to the lumpy stone walls, mushrooms and ivy lining the walls and floors, and some barred off cells on the darkest side, riddled with vines and thorns all of which looked less than inviting, by their gleaming sanguine hues, suggesting, to Nej, a poisonous nature. A steady dripping sound emanated from within the overgrowth.

To her left, opposite the malevolent garden enclosure was a narrow stone staircase, next to which sat her lone guard, on a low wooden stool, whittling a piece of soft wood with a small knife. At that moment he looked at her, meeting her gaze, then glanced at his knife and rose with a smirk, but before he could approach her with whatever evil intent had played in his mind, there were footfalls on the stone staircase. He sheathed the knife at his belt and tossed the wood aside as the Queen herself arrived, encompassed by a hefty entourage of bodyguards. She marched up before Nej and stood proudly, defiantly, with her hands on her hips, glaring down upon her.

"You don't deserve the opportunity to speak," the Queen began, abrasively. "Murdering one of our people, as witnessed by his fellow soldier—there is no doubt of your guilt and your purpose in coming here. And so you shall be put to death, your corpse displayed at the edge of our lands for our enemies to see."

The Queen turned to go. Nej had to do something. She closed her eyes and murmured a short chant, and a brilliant burst of light erupted from her, filling the room, leaving a sparkle on the walls and entities which slowly began to fade. It was enough to make the Queen, and everyone, halt and stare in wonder around them. The Queen looked back at Nej with interest.

"I am not your enemy," Nej quietly insisted.

* * *

The Queen allowed Nej an audience in her throne room, though she exuded skepticism.

"You allege that you did not murder one of my subjects. Yet a loyal soldier, a veteran who has earned rewards for his valor, speaks otherwise. Your...*unique* ability intrigues me, as, to the best of my knowledge, it is foreign to the Koi'Tan. This is the only reason I will hear your words. If our enemies in this civil war have discovered new magic, it is essential that I learn its nature, for the safety of my people and success of our dispute."

Nej took a deep breath. "M'lady," she began at last, "I am not of your clan. As I have tried to explain, I am from the H'nomi, a group of nomadic magic-users, healers, seeking a peaceful home beyond the feuding clans and golems spread across our continent.

"I did not harm your subject; rather I found him unconscious. I have no desire to harm anyone—it is not the nature of my magic. While I am capable with a blade and bow, I do not use violence except in defense, and even then I seek to avoid it. If I may demonstrate," Nej placed her right hand over her left arm, where a large burn mark lingered. Closing her eyes, a soft glow emanated from her hand and the mark faded and disappeared in moments. She glanced back at the Queen, who looked faintly impressed.

She made a motion then, and from behind where Nej knelt there came the footsteps of the cavern guards.

"Vai'shun," the Queen said sharply, as several soldiers came to a halt beside Nej, "I have a doubt."

Vai'shun looked unfazed.

"She might be able to heal, my Queen, but she is equally capable of inflicting wounds, as I myself witnessed."

"Vai'shun," snapped the Queen in anger. "Koi'Tan do not posses this magical knowledge to heal by touch alone! She is not of our clan, be it Loyalist or Separatist, and that much should have been evident upon her appearance! You found her struggling through the jungle, as only a foreigner would.

"You have lied to me. About her, about the death of one of our own—your comrade, implicating an innocent person knowing it would bring about her demise, when you, in fact, being the only other individual present, must have taken his life yourself.

"In doing this you have made me look a fool for misplacing my trust in you.

"Any *one* of these transgressions would be unforgivable. But the combination—" the Queen's words faltered as she attempted to maintain her composure. Her rage was infallible.

"You are a traitor who does not even deserve death. I shall deliver you in chains to our enemy to do with as they please. After breaking your arms and removing your tongue so you can deal no more treachery."

The man paled in shock, realizing the gravity of his actions, stunned that the Queen believed this foreigner over him.

"M'lady," Nej said again, very softly, feeling uncomfortable with the harshness of the Queen's sentence, "May I ask you to pardon, Vai'shun..." The Queen stared at her in disbelief, and

Nej gulped before continuing.

"His actions may be inexcusable among your people. But I believe a person can learn from their mistakes, and I believe in forgiveness. Perhaps, he suspected me to be an enemy spy, and when you gave me a chance, he thought he was protecting you, and all your people, by finding a way to have me confined.

"While his preconception was misguided, his intent was just. I wish to change his opinion of me, and perhaps he can help me with my quest. Furthermore when I leave this jungle I will be in great need of a guide, and he would serve very well, if you would have no more use for him here."

The Queen pondered. "It is not our way to show leniency. But I see it is yours. As you have a need for his services, he will be at your disposal. But when you have left here, see that he never returns, or he will find only his end among the Koi'Tan." Her eyes bore into Vai'shun as she spoke these words, and he looked away with equal intensity.

Nej bowed her head, "Thank you, M'lady."

"And so," continued the Queen with some hostility, "Why *have* you come here?"

"I am grateful for this opportunity to speak with you," Nej said, "For I have a request which only you might fulfill, and I fear you will not desire to do so.

"Long ago, our clans were united as one tribe, until the fall of a great tree. With the end of that tree, at the hands of several young friends, came the end of peace. Since that time we have wandered this continent separately, always fighting, always afraid. When the tree was destroyed, so too was an object; the destructors each took a fragment of the object, then parted ways, each followed by the beginning of their new clans. It is said these fragments were passed down among the leaders of each clan. I am here asking for the Koi'Tan fragment. I wish to reunite all the fragments and use them to heal the great tree, and in doing so heal this land which is slowly decaying from the place where the tree lies dying.

"You have your clan, and that will not change. I will ask no one to join me. But allow me and any who, of their own free will, desire to return to the tree, to do so, and finally find peace again."

The Queen smiled slightly as she paced before her throne.

"It is interesting that this is your request. For that fragment is the very cause of our civil war." She gazed at Nej. "It makes one question your veracity. Perhaps this truly is another ploy by Hervana to steal what is mine; what was my sister's before me." She glowered at Nej, studying Nej's reaction.

"I understand, M'lady. You have no reason to believe me, especially given your circumstances." Nej paused a moment in thought. "What, may I ask," she said slowly, "Would be the result if Hervana was to acquire the fragment you possess?"

The Queen smiled again, playing along, though still uncertain if Nej was merely creating an elaborate ruse.

"Whoever has the fragment will win in any battle. And whoever has the fragment is recognized as the true ruler of Koi'Tan. Even though the Separatists, rebels, follow Hervana now, it is only because they believe she did steal the fragment when she murdered my sister. What she holds is fake and she knows it. But she cannot let that be known to the rest or they will not follow her. She has been desperate since she discovered the truth to get her hands on the real fragment."

"How did she realize it was fake?" Nej pressed.

"There was a significant battle in which we engaged, seasons ago, before the rains. She believed it would be my undoing, and at last an opportunity for her to overwhelm me and take over as the true leader of all our people. But her forces were driven back and back, until she began to see she could not possibly hold the fragment. Such devastation the fragment does not allow. She was forced to retreat and I do not know how she explained the loss to her followers. Since that time, some have slowly come back to us, but we never fully trust them—as we did not trust you."

"Most compelling," Nej voiced aloud, as her thoughts raced. No wonder no clan eliminated another. It would seem the H'nomi should be very weak, and yet they continually stood up to the Entari and Tayuuk. A few would perish in each battle, but each clan as a whole persevered, because each clan bore a magical fragment from the tree.

"You are here, protected from the fighting in the north," Nej explained, "But my people must continually fight other clans. Now I see how we manage to live. The luck of a crystal fragment."

"How do you know it is a crystal?" the Queen interjected, immediately suspicious.

"I don't," Nej admitted, "But I suppose it was how I imagined it when I was first told the story. A glowing gem is how I see it, which grew dark when shattered. What else could be broken in such a way? Perhaps it is, however, more of a seed; a glowing seed...

"One could ponder eternally but I admit I have never seen one of these fragments myself. You are the second leader to speak of it. The first was Fier'lor of the Tayuuk, who claimed 'there is a part in all of us which belongs to something'—the 'us' referring to the leaders of each clan."

This time the Queen seemed pleased with her words. "This is true. It is not a fragment which can be handed off, like a shard of a crystal, as Hervana believes. It is a part within. Each leader is a living Boikk tree, in a sense. And this is how the clans will never reunite, and how only the new leader retains the knowledge of the legend and of the fragment.

"Only through the death of the leader can the part be extracted. And so, you see, your request cannot be fulfilled."

Nej felt her heart sink at these words. A chill ran through her as she wondered how she could carry out her dream in light of this unprecedented information.

"Now go, and rest, and perhaps in the morning light, Vai'shun can escort you from our jungle. I regret that we cannot aid you further."

With a wave of her hand the Queen dismissed Nej and Vai'shun, and a pair of guards escorted them away to a small room bearing two beds and a table, with a wash bin and some victuals. There was an open, organic-shaped window high up between the two beds. The doorway too was unsealed, and the two guards took up posts at either side of it. Vai'shun sat on one bed and stared out the window, looking melancholy, but with some fierceness lingering in his eyes.

Nej was deeply dismayed and needed someone to talk to. She couldn't let her quest end like this. She wished Zuun were with her; he would probably have a brilliant idea. Maybe even be able to extract the fragment without killing the host. What could this fragment be?

"Vai'shun...Sir," Nej whispered. He shifted slightly, but wouldn't look at her. "Will you help me?" she asked. Now he did look to her, in annoyance.

"Help you? Help you to what, kill the Queen? As was your plan all along? Look where you've landed me. I've no mind to help you at all. I'll get you lost in the jungle and once the Vitherpire or Shoksage have eaten you I'll be free to do as I please. Join some other clan and become leader of it and live for decades…"

He stopped short. In his anger he'd said too much, he realized. He seemed to do that: go too far.

"I have no desire to kill anyone, Sir. I never did. I just wish there was some way to revive the tree. But it seems the only way is to bring all the leaders there. Or all the fragments.

"It isn't by chance in their very blood? There isn't a way to take so little it would not be missed, and have it translate into a part of the fragment?"

Vai'shun smirked. "You really want this." He gave a deep sigh, then chuckled while running a hand through his hair. "Look, I really don't know any other way," then he moved forward and motioned her closer, glancing at the entryway where the guards stood, eavesdropping for sure. When she was close he whispered, "But I have seen the fragment. I was there with Tiore when her sister died; when the fragment passed between them. Her sister, Niahla, always wore a crystal around her neck, so everyone would assume that was the notorious fragment of legend. But Tiore alone knew differently. I'll never forget how she coaxed the…*thing*…from her sister's dying body. Of course, it desires to live, so it attaches to something living."

Nej realized her revulsion must be showing on her face and she attempted to shake it away.

"This gets more complicated every moment," she murmured.

"So this *thing* is alive?" she added.

"Not so keen to get mixed up in it after all, are you," Vai'shun gloated, clearly still sore at the nasty predicament 'she' had caused.

"I did not expect this," she admitted in discouragement. "And I do not wish to endanger your Queen, or any of your people, in taking the fragment from you. What trouble it might cause your people in this war. I must think on this."

Looking to Vai'shun, she concluded, "Thank you for the information."

CHAPTER 9
The First Fragment

Night had fallen, and Vai'shun was silent and still in his bed. After spending many minutes fully healing her injuries, Nej laid on her bed, exhausted—but couldn't sleep; she was vexed with the thought that in the morning she would be forced to leave, losing what might be her only chance to change her world.

She had to speak with the Queen again. She propped herself up slightly, glancing toward the doorway where the shadows of the guards danced in the torchlight. She heard their gentle whispers as they entertained themselves with conversation. Occasionally one would let out a muted chuckle. Moving slowly, Nej slipped noiselessly off her bed and tiptoed across the room, just a couple of steps, to where Vai'shun lay.

She took a little breath, wondering how she could wake him without startling him. Suddenly there was a shout from somewhere in the palace halls, and the sound of rushing feet, and jostling about; further yells and movement were audible from beyond the walls, in the village. The guards disappeared from their posts, and Vai'shun rolled over and looked at her with narrowed eyes.

She held up her hands innocently. "It isn't what you think," she whispered. She stepped backward to give him space. He sat up and tossed his legs over the side of his bed.

"That so?" he remarked, glaring at her a moment more before rising and listening to the sounds around them.

"What's happening," he demanded.

"I—I don't know," Nej stammered, "I was about to try to wake you when the village sprang to life, and our guards vanished."

"Bet anything it's an attack," Vai'shun muttered, as he strode to the window and paused a few moments, examining the village through the opening. Turning back to Nej he asked, "And why did you want to wake me?"

"I...need your help, again. I need to speak with the Queen once more."

Vai'shun chuckled. "Persistent," he remarked with a shake of his head. "Let's find Tiore, and determine the cause of this commotion. We help her with this, and she might hear you out."

A guard himself, Vai'shun took action, moving to the doorway and scanning quickly in both directions. "Let's go," he ordered, and hurried into the corridor. Nej followed, closely and silently.

They skirted deftly down the passage toward the throne room; at the first intersection they hugged the wall in the darkness as several soldiers thumped by. After they passed, Vai'shun and Nej followed them to the throne room and peeked into the entry.

"Report!" the Queen announced, having entered the chamber from another exit, hidden behind some vines at the back of the cavern.

A guard stepped forward. "Separatists have entered the village, my Queen. By the time the eastern watchtower alerted us to their presence, they were at our gates."

The Queen scowled in annoyance. "Was the guard asleep? How could he be so slow to detect them!

"Get out there and push them back!" she all but shouted. The guards bowed to the Queen, but before they could turn around Vai'shun grabbed Nej's hand and dragged her down the corridor and hid with her behind the nearest corner.

Once the guards had raced past them again, Vai'shun escorted Nej to the throne room, where the Queen was just retreating toward the hidden passage.

Vai'shun strode boldly through the entrance and announced, "My Queen."

Tiore spun around in surprise, her eyes wide as she glanced between her visitors.

Vai'shun dropped to a knee, bowing his head, and Nej followed suit. "My Queen," Vai'shun repeated more softly, "Permit us to aid in protecting your village and your people. You will not regret it."

Tiore approached them with eyes narrowed, doubtful after the events which had unfolded.

"Very strange indeed, that this night the Separatists invade," she mused.

"Is it mere coincidence, that it occurs only after my trusted bodyguard betrays his people and his Queen?"

"Tiore," Vai'shun looked at the Queen, and she seemed startled, but not incredibly annoyed by his informality. "I did not kill Ruvar. I accused this foreigner, perhaps mistakenly, of his death, but it was not my hand that slayed him."

The Queen looked pleased, but still skeptical. She looked to Nej. "Too much hiding; one questions what to believe. And I begin to distrust you as well, dear girl."

Nej, not overly surprised by Vai'shun's revelation, quickly supported his entreaties, saying, "M'lady, your concern is natural, but misplaced. Your village is overrun with your enemies, but we are not among them. We only ask for one more chance to prove ourselves."

"Our guards have left their posts," Vai'shun added. "We could have left at our will and joined the enemy if that was our goal. Or we could have fled; taken our freedom. Tiore, I've protected and supported you all your life. I don't intend to stop now."

A smile toyed on Tiore's lips, and she gave a brief nod.

"Be gone then; you have my permission and authority to act as necessary to preserve my people."

Vai'shun rose and bowed to the Queen, then, turning, took Nej's hand and pulled her to her feet. Keeping a firm but gentle grip on her hand, he escorted her out of the cavern once more.

Vai'shun lead the way out of the palace and into the streets of the village. Shouts, footsteps, and the clashing of wood and stone and metal echoed all around them. Torches blazed and shadows flickered on the stone walls. As they reached the end of one alley, a man suddenly fell to the ground before them. He brandished his sword above him as two enemies swung their own weapons downward. Nej pulled her hand from Vai'shun's and thrust a magical shield over the fallen man. Vai'shun looked at her, and whispered, "That is one of our enemies."

Nej glared at him and spoke loudly, "Your enemies were once your own clan! Your civil war must end, as must the continental battle. Don't you know, we are all of the same blood."

The fallen soldier scrambled to his feet, unsure at first if he should run or stay. He glanced at his two pursuers, however, still blocked by Nej's shield, and nervously fled in the opposite direction.

There was a shout from another section of town and the two Loyalists raced toward the new commotion.

"You're right," Vai'shun admitted, as Nej lowered her hands, dissolving the shield.

"This has to end. Tonight."

Nej gave a slight smile.

"Let's see how bad things are and if we can push them back," Vai'shun added, and lead again through the maze of village streets.

He entered a narrow, yet tall square building, and climbed a series of ladders inside up to the third level, which had an open balcony. From here they looked down upon the village, at the fighting throughout the streets. It looked like chaos to Nej, but Vai'shun immediately pointed, saying, "There!"

Nej's eyes followed his finger. She saw a pale figure, in a shimmering silvery robe fighting amongst the otherwise primarily tan-colored soldiers, all pushing through a broken gate into the village. "The woman?" Nej asked.

Vai'shun nodded.

"That's Hervana. She's here—for the fragment," he looked knowingly at Nej.

Nej took in a deep breath, watching those amassed at the gate.

"It seems few have gotten far into the city," she observed.

Vai'shun scanned the rest of the village and replied with relief, "Only a handful of scouts scaled the walls; they've already been apprehended; but this is their true force, lead by Hervana."

"Vai'shun," he turned to face her, and saw she was gazing sadly at the fighting below. "Now is the time for your war to end. If I take the fragment, Hervana will have nothing left to fight for. But it must happen now, while she's in the city."

Vai'shun looked concerned, but gave a nod of affirmation.

"Alright. Let's return to Tiore."

* * *

They maneuvered swiftly back through the now mostly empty streets, the soldiers primarily occupied at the break-in point, and any civilians unwilling or unable to fight, barricaded inside their homes.

Finding the throne room deserted, Vai'shun directed Nej to the hidden exit leading to Tiore's own quarters. They passed an enchanting, vine and flower-riddled hall into her elaborate living area.

Tiore whirled when she heard their steps; she was dressed in armor, preparing for battle.

"You return so soon?"

Vai'shun glanced at Nej, awaiting her explanation.

"Your Highness," Nej began, stepping forward, "Hervana is leading the attack on your village. While we *could* simply push them back, I propose we instead end your war, by taking away the item she seeks. If there is no longer a fragment to determine the ruler, then the ruler must be selected by other means, and the people will collectively align behind that single leader. You war will be over, Your Highness. My taking the fragment will bring peace for your people, and I will then use the fragment to bring peace to mine."

Tiore scowled. "The leader *always* bears the fragment! It has been handed down among the rulers to remind us of why the tree was destroyed in the first place!"

Approaching Nej, Tiore continued, "Because the tree was too strong. It controlled us all. Even this small fragment is much too powerful to even be removed until after death. It is embedded within..." She absently touched her chest, glancing away.

Nej moved nearer and touched Tiore's arm gently.

"I can remove it," she assured. "The tree has spoken to me, and I believe I am meant to create this change. I must try.

"The tree is powerful, yes," Nej continued, "but also necessary. The land is dying from the point of the damaged tree. Soon it will consume our entire continent and we will have nowhere to live. You may stay here in your jungle; but without the tree, even the jungle will soon be destroyed. Please let me try to save us all." She allowed some of her magic to flow into Tiore, creating a sense of soothing, and Tiore stared at her, considering.

"Perhaps you can," Tiore admitted. "If the tree has contacted you, then your link to the tree and these fragments may be strong enough. Others have tried and failed...but I have seen your magic, and I will allow you to try."

Tiore untied and removed her gleaming golden breastplate, then placed a hand over her chest. "It lies here."

Nej took in a deep breath and reached out, feeling the energy of the fragment, and of the very air around them. Her hands began to glow green and the same glow showed on Tiore's skin. Tiore winced, and Nej's brow furrowed and she put out her other hand, sending a white energy toward Tiore, a healing light, while mentally drawing the fragment away. Vai'shun stared in wonder as a small lump slowly emerged through Tiore's skin, which Nej concurrently healed as the fragment was extracted. At last Nej stopped the healing spell, and held in her right hand, the green-tinted bit of seed. Already it was growing shoots, searching for something to cling to; to embed itself within a life form once again.

Vai'shun and Tiore looked at it in shock. Nej was terrified by the living form she held. She placed it against her left wrist, and allowed it to connect to her, cringing as it penetrated her skin. Again she healed the spot where it entered, and Tiore said, "Here," She hurried to a chest, rummaged inside and drew out a thin leather bracer, engraved with various tribal symbols. Tiore tied it to Nej's wrist, covering the fragment.

"Now you will go?" Tiore asked.

Nej replied, "I believe it is best that I do, so this fragment cannot fall into your enemy's hands, and so you can at last end your war."

Tiore nodded. Nej glanced at Vai'shun.

"I will see you safely out of the jungle," he promised. Nej smiled and turned back to Tiore.

"Thank you, Your Highness. And *Saal'tai-yt:* Good blessings upon you." Tiore nodded absently, looking deep in thought. Perhaps she was affected by the sudden and unexpected removal of the fragment, Nej thought. Perhaps it had given her extra strength after all. But there was not time to waste. Nej and Vai'shun moved toward the exit, when Tiore softly called, "One more thing, Nej—

"The fragments do form a seed, but not one which you plant in the ground. Remember, this seed was found within the tree, not buried in the dirt. It is more akin to...a heart."

Nej gazed at her a moment, then gave a bow and departed the Queen's chambers.

Their escape was not so effortless as they hoped. When they entered the village streets again, they found them overrun with Separatists. Vai'shun drew his sword and fought alongside his fellow soldiers. Nej attempted to keep them healed and shielded.

They gradually inched away from the invaders, retreating down dark alleys until they reached an empty guard tower behind the palace cave. They climbed the ladders inside to the upper level and searched from high for a path out of the village.

Vai'shun breathed, "Tiore."

And there she was, fighting her way with grace and finesse toward Hervana. Wearing slender golden armor and wielding two dancing sais, Tiore looked like a warrior princess. Hervana, in her flowing silvery robe, swinging a long glowing white blade, appeared more like a priestess. Nej supposed that might be her intention; to deter attacks by appearing almost holy.

"Tiore will need my protection," Vai'shun said ruefully. "I must go down to her."

"She looks capable," Nej remarked, as Tiore effortlessly maneuvered through the soldiers.

Vai'shun spun toward her, and Nej was surprised by the anger in his face.

"Tiore has never fought without the fragment. And Hervana does not fight fairly. Nor will Hervana believe Tiore is on her own."

"Yes—yes," Nej agreed hastily. "Go, of course; I didn't mean that you should not do precisely as you feel is best." She glanced down at the two enemies, who had now caught sight of one another and were advancing.

"Should I join you?" she asked, but Vai'shun was already gone.

* * *

Vai'shun tore through the streets, his blade a stinging breeze as it sliced through the air, clearing his way to his Queen.

Hervana and Tiore had finally met. Tiore yelled, "Let all observe!"

Nearby fighting slowed, and Loyalist and Separatist members

gathered behind their respective leaders. Vai'shun arrived just in time, blocking some Separatists with his sword and a shake of his head when they moved as if to attack the Loyalist leader; they instead stepped back and lowered their weapons. Vai'shun glanced to Tiore, then continually scanned the crowd as she spoke, assuring her safety.

Once she had their attention, Tiore monologued:

"I am Queen Tiore, rightful ruler of the Koi'Tan. Hervana, vying for my title and position, committed treason, murdering my sister and deceiving many of my people with her lies.

"Always, our people have been ruled by the one who bears the ancient fragment from the Boikk tree. A fragment which gives great power and protection. Hervana has never seen nor touched this fragment! She is no leader! She is a fraud and a coward.

"Let Hervana and I duel, and let the winner have the allegiance of all. Let our pointless war end, when one of us is slain at last. I shall avenge my sister's death, and claim my right to rule all Koi'Tan."

There were cheers on both sides, but Hervana's face had paled. A chorus of shouts erupted, from both sides:

"Show her she's wrong Hervana!"

"Hervana's the true leader!"

"Down with the traitor!"

"Well, Hervana?" Tiore said coyly. Hervana tightened her grip on her sword, narrowing her eyes.

"I will defend my honor against your denunciation. I will fight for the fragment. A ruler should not be chosen based on her ancestry, but by her actions, her wisdom, her strength. I deserve to be Queen, not you. And in defeating you I will prove it."

Tiore smiled evilly, then lunged at Hervana. Hervana wasn't prepared for the sudden attack; she tried to block with her sword and spin away, but one sai gouged her side. There was a gasp from the crowd, and Hervana cried out, but the wound was small, and she immediately lashed back with her sword, cutting down in waves toward Tiore, who was forced to backpedal, repeatedly blocking the attacks as they came.

Seeing she was nearing the crowd, Tiore at last ducked and tumbled out of the way, leaving Hervana unbalanced as she swung at empty air. Tiore leapt again from partly behind Hervana and sliced across her back. Hervana moved too slowly to defend the first attack, but blocked the second which came from below and managed to fling aside one of Tiore's sais. Tiore smirked, and Hervana glared at her, in pain from the points where blood had been drawn.

Little did she know, the first strike had already won the battle for Tiore. For Tiore faithfully coated her weapons with a deadly poison, though it took some time for its effect to transpire. As Hervana looked at her, a trace of fear flashed in her eyes. She felt a strange weakness spreading across her body. In that moment she knew. But she didn't give up.

Tiore was surprised by Hervana's strength and speed as she advanced, striking from every angle, leaving nicks on Tiore's calves and arms where Tiore was unable to evade in time.

Hervana's blade, too, was unique. A pernicious compound created the ethereal white glow it exhibited. Her alchemists had experimented with a variety of plants, and eventually found a working combination. This particular mixture included a sparkling mushroom-like growth with a natural glow, which could cause shock and paralysis, as well as a hot, white pepper which grew in rare clusters in the hottest, humid southern reaches of the jungle where steam vents and natural saunas were found. This pepper burned the skin to touch. These and other plants were crushed and affixed to the blade, leaving it with a permanent glowing crystalline texture. Perhaps more importantly, each strike would cause lingering burns to the skin, and had the potential to weaken with various stages of paralysis, depending on the location and depth of the wound.

And so Tiore felt her muscles slowing; she was unable to dodge as quickly, and each additional injury she was unfortunate enough to acquire only decreased her agility further. The cuts also hurt more than she anticipated, and she too realized Hervana had done something to her own blade. She hoped it wasn't too late for her, as it was for Hervana.

Hervana struck once more across Tiore's right arm, giving a solid gouge this time, then fell to her knees on the ground, looking ill. Tiore knew the poison was now taking effect. Hervana glared up at her.

"You cheat," she whispered.

Tiore laughed.

"And you?" Tiore tried to lift her blade to strike, but suddenly, her arm wasn't moving. Hervana saw the confusing on her face and smirked, then summoned all her strength to deliver a quick but deep slice across Tiore's chest, knowing Tiore would be unable to block it now. Both women fell to the ground then, though Hervana expired first.

Vai'shun was at Tiore's side instantly, trying to tend the wounds.

"You've won," he assured her, hoping to give her the will to hold on.

She looked at him haughtily. "Of course I won. But if I had that fragment..." She winced and took a strained breath. The paralysis was spreading to her lungs, and heart.

Suddenly Nej was there. She too knelt beside Tiore and lifted her hands over her, trying to heal her. But this effect, much like the Tayuuk's magic on her mind, was foreign to her, and her magic couldn't understand it. "Don't you have something to combat this?" she asked desperately. Closing her eyes, she focused the energy of the fragment toward Tiore, trying to restore life.

But Tiore broke her concentration.

"You," she said vilely, "You have brought my death. I could not be killed as long as I had the fragment inside me.

"All of you!" she called to her people, her voice breaking and weak as she struggled to breathe. Vai'shun reached out instinctively to support her. "This outsider has taken the fragment and caused the death of your Queen! She should be punished, and as my dying wish I command you to see that she suffers a fate no better than mine."

Murmurs spread over the crowd, and a couple of the Queen's soldiers grabbed Nej's arms and dragged her away from Tiore. Others encroached upon Nej, weapons ready to deal out the Queen's orders.

"No," Vai'shun said, his firm, steady voice resonating in the silence. Everyone looked back at him, and saw the Queen had passed, as he laid her still form on the ground and rose to his feet.

"It's over," Vai'shun continued. "The two women who created and continued this feud amongst us are gone. We have no more reason to fight. And this girl, Nej, has a greater purpose. She is taking the fragment away, to heal the Boikk tree, and restore our lands to the health and life they once had.

"If you were to go beyond the jungle, as I have, you would see that only desolation lies there. That same death will come here as well, if left unchecked. We must think of the greater good, and allow her to leave."

The soldiers holding Nej looked at each other, then released her.

"But who will rule?" someone called out.

Vai'shun gazed across the crowd.

"It is time for change. For the Koi'Tan to choose a leader who they can trust, because of her wisdom and integrity, not because she wields some ancient seed—perhaps blessed, perhaps cursed, we know not. Hervana was right in this," he looked pointedly at the Separatists, who seemed pleased.

"I say we select a ruler from amongst ourselves. Those willing to lead step forward. Those willing to follow, join your leader."

No one moved. They looked at one another, and at the ground, and at Vai'shun. There was nudging, and shaking of heads.

Nej said softly, "I think you would be a great leader, Vai'shun."

Voices of affirmation followed, sentiments which grew louder and stronger, until one soldier said, "Well Vai'shun?"

"What title should he have?" someone else shouted out, and the crowd erupted again.

Vai'shun lifted his hands for silence.

"I would be honored to lead our clan. And I would like to follow suit of the other clans, and lead as your Chief. King, is too strong a word. We have no need for such powerful rulers. We are a strong people, and a cunning people, and now we will work together, to better ourselves, and better our world."

Everyone cheered, and Vai'shun lifted a hand again.

"Thank you, all, but there is some unfinished business here.

"Our former leaders deserve a proper burial, and proper respect and mourning."

He motioned, and several came to take away the deceased.

"And any who require medical care, please follow T'nak," he placed a hand on the shoulder of a tall, bearded Loyalist soldier. "He will direct you to our infirmary."

Vai'shun turned to Nej.

"There is much work to be done here. But you must be on your way. You will require an escort out of the jungle—"

Nej smiled.

"I believe I can manage, Vai'shun. Thank you for all your

help."

Vai'shun frowned. "You weren't managing very well when I found you."

Nej laughed. "Maybe I've learned since then. Besides I have the fragment. I'll be alright, Vai'shun, though I appreciate your concern.

"And, if you'd like to see the results of our efforts, please, meet me, and whoever else will join us, at the site of the Boikk tree—at daybreak, after four nights time. I hope to acquire the remaining fragments by then, and reunite them before members of all the clans."

"I will. I will lead as many as wish to come, to see this restoration. It will start a new chapter for all our clans, and hopefully bring a time of peace and unification.

"Nej. Thank you for coming to the Koi'Tan. You bring kindness and understanding wherever you go. You will change the world."

Nej wrapped her arms around the new Chief of the Koi'Tan. "See you soon, Vai'shun," she said, feeling enormously happy to have a new friend. As she turned to go, her mind drifted to her other friends, specifically Zuun, wondering where he was and what he had accomplished since they separated.

Chapter 10
The Second Fragment

Zuun caught up with his golem.

"Didn't think I'd let you go without me, did you?" he grinned broadly.

"I am always pleased to have your company, Zuun," the golem responded. "But do you not think there is great danger if we come across hostile golems together?"

"Of course there is," Zuun agreed, "But that isn't our only task. Let's return to our village first and gather fresh supplies. And a little something extra."

After a lengthy and tedious trek across the desert, most of which was passed by the golem, at a run, with Zuun on his back, they reached the small Zenuran encampment. It was late in the day, the sun setting and darkness impending. The pair went first to their hut, allowing Zuun to gather victuals, water, and some mechanical parts and devices, all of which he tossed into a ragged leather sack.

"Alright Jett, next we need to see Vierux."

"Hah, Hah," Jett said in perfect mock laughter.

"What, you don't think she'll see me?" Zuun grinned and patted his friend on the arm. They moved through the dusty torch-lit streets, making their way to the larger structure in the center of the village. This was the palace, if it could be called that, from which their desert princess reigned. She was very young, younger than Zuun, but had ruled for a few years, since the passing of her grandfather. Vierux was his only living relative, and he had been her caregiver since her parents death from a golem battle when she was just an infant.

As they approached the fabric-draped doorway, a guard in front blocked their path with his staff and commanded, "State your purpose."

Zuun cleared his throat.

"I will be leaving, into golem territory, tonight, and would like to have a few words with our leader before departing, in case she would like me to scout somewhere in particular, or has any other needs beyond our village walls."

Zuun was pleased with himself. He thought this a very fitting explanation. The look on Jett's mechanical visage was a mock play on boredom and skepticism. His surprise was equally evident when the guard pulled aside his staff and gave a jerk of his head, allowing them inside. Fortunately, most Zenura didn't observe golem behaviors unless they were hostile, believing them, as mere constructs, incapable of emotion. How foolish, Zuun thought, that the very air of superiority that caused them to be destroyed by their own creations in the first place, lingered even after they had been proven wrong. Would they ever learn?

They hurried inside and heard fighting sounds; they saw a young girl sparring with an older, armored man, Zuun presumed a trainer. The young girl was aggressive and fierce; her youth gave her a rebellious, overconfident attitude, but in regards to her fighting skill, this attitude was not unworthy.

Zuun hadn't seen Vierux for years—not up close like this, and not for any length of time. He had played with her as a child; they had been friends for nearly ten years prior, when his mother would sometimes care for and instruct groups of village children. Every once in awhile, however, they were plagued by a golem attack, and since the one that took his mother, he'd never interacted with Vierux again.

It had been of no consequence to him before; he was not interested in her or any other Zenurans. His studies and his golem, his own experiments and inventions, occupied all his time and concern. Such was the mindset of many Zenuran engineers. But now, he suddenly found something else to draw his attention.

Vierux had deep olive skin, naturally tanned and smooth, and very long pale ash blonde hair, tapering thick and soft over her shoulders and down her back. Her eyes were dark, perhaps black or brown or violet, but too dark to tell, and very large. She was short and slender, tough yet alluring. Zuun was enraptured. Nej had been studious, kind, patient and mature, much like his mother, and he felt an immediate kinship; but this was much different.

The princess finished her fight, nodded to the trainer, who left the room, as she sheathed her dagger and stared a moment, inspecting Zuun.

"What do you want," she said at last, retreating to her throne, where she slumped in an apathetic pose. A bronze-hued desert fox that had been perched on the back of the throne hopped down onto Vierux' lap where she scratched its soft fur. Zuun was forced to remind himself of the plan he'd concocted for the guard.

Stepping closer, Zuun said, "I am leaving the village, and traveling into golem country. I came to ask if there is anything you need beyond our walls."

She gave a suspicious laugh. "Is that so," she said. It wasn't a question.

"Also I have a friend," he continued, realizing she didn't buy his lie as easily as her guard, "Who wishes to…change the world." Vierux rose an eyebrow.

"We've gone to the site of the Boikk tree. The one from the old songs and stories. And it…doesn't look good."

"How so?" she asked, being young enough to be interested, and rebellious enough to no longer care about the reasons the old had for splitting up the original tribe. Besides, she remembered Zuun's mother's teachings too, and was always fascinated with her tales of the old tree and its lush surroundings. The desert was dry, barren—boring.

Encouraged by Vierux's interest, Zuun continued.

"The land is dying all around the tree, and it seems to be spreading. We believe, if left to continue, the entire continent will become a wasteland. We want to heal the tree. But we need a few things to do it." He looked at her knowingly; a gaze she returned.

"I see," she said at last.

Giving her fox one last stroke she moved it to the ground and rose unexpectedly, saying softly, "Come with me."

As they walked she glanced back at his golem.

"Is he safe?" she remarked uncertainly. Zuun nodded.

"He's my best friend," he smiled with pride. She smirked.

She led the way to an isolated room at the back of the palace. A curtained-off bed was at one side, and a desk riddled with metal and cloth scraps and gems and devices on another side. Little trinkets and books lined shelves while strange objects dangled from the ceiling and walls. It was mesmerizing.

"A few of my own inventions," she explained, gesturing at the elaborate display. "The object you seek, is a piece of the tree, correct? I have experimented with it significantly. My grandfather wore it on him, as he said all the leaders did and had for generations. It granted immunity from death, he said. It kept our people alive. I thought, how could it protect all, if it's attached to just one. And he, my grandfather, still died, so it doesn't grant eternal life—just some sort of extra strength. For it is true he never died in any battles; though my parents did." There was a note of bitterness in her voice. She turned sharply to Zuun.

"I thought, I could do more. We can. Why do we continue to be ravaged by golems. Forced to waste away in this monotonous desert. What good is our livelihood? There must be more."

Zuun smiled. "Exactly how we feel," he assured her.

She approached a fountain, beneath the window of her room. It was an exquisite fountain, riddled with all manner of small plants and ferns and flowers, blossoming and growing, spreading through the entire room. Vines reached everywhere and hung across the doorway, creating a barrier. He realized the curtain over the bed was actually plant life. He noted the fox's glowing eyes from where it rested on the bed, watching him like a guard. He quickly looked away. Glancing past the window he saw the green even extended beyond, creating a garden behind the palace. It was beautiful. "How long has this—How did—"

She smiled at him. "A garden in the desert? How can it be?" she read his thoughts. Reaching through the water of the fountain, she ran a hand from the top down, and several lights flashed and the metal opened, revealing a glowing...something, inside. Zuun squinted through the flowing water.

"Here is your fragment. It prefers to be affixed to something living. But I convinced it to sustain itself here instead. I don't fancy having a foreign life form attached to my skin."

Zuun cringed at the thought and said, "I don't blame you," and added, "This is incredible!

"If you could do this much, with just one fragment—give life to the desert—imagine what we could do with all the fragments together! We could restore the tree and the entire continent. The whole place could be this beautiful."

Vierux smiled. "I'm glad someone appreciates it."

"You're a talented botanical engineer," Zuun praised. "I've never seen anything like it."

"It's still a work in progress," she admitted. "Seeing what the fragment is capable of, and how we can improve our conditions. I was hoping I could also find a way to use it to guarantee our safety from the golems, in time."

"But you'll help me?" Zuun said. "Can we take it from here, take it back to the tree? We need all five fragments together or it won't work."

Vierux sighed. "Of course I am intrigued by your idea, and I support your desire. But what of our people? And what of the legend? The original clan leaders destroyed the tree for a reason. Will the clans all agree now that they made a mistake?"

"It's dying, Vierux," he said, "And everything around it is dying too. I think the tree is what made our entire world alive. We can still have separate clans, and live in separate places, but without the tree, nothing else can exist. We need to fix it now, or it might become too late."

She considered. "You may be right," she agreed. "The founders shouldn't have destroyed the tree. But they thought it was the only way to gain a following. They thought no one would listen to them if they didn't…insist."

She gazed at Zuun. "Alright. But you said you wished to leave tonight—unfortunately we cannot proceed so soon.

"As I said, I prefer not to allow the seed to attach to me. And so it must have some sort of transport, a safe carriage in which it can continue living."

"You think it'll die, just being on it's own for a few days?"

"Do you really want to risk that? To the best of my knowledge, it must be attached to something growing to stay alive, and I know I don't want it touching me."

"Alright…we hold off on our journey until the seed is ready. But I'm supposed to meet my friend at dawn, after five nights. And I still have to find and somehow convince the golems to help us—"

"Golems!" Vierux interrupted.

"Yes, we're going to need their aid—"

Vierux waved a hand impatiently. "Enough talk. I understand you're in a hurry. But this must be done correctly. You may explain all the details once I've determined how to create a portable container."

"How can I help?"

CHAPTER 11
Return to the H'nomi

It was very late when Nej left the safety of the village and passed into the surrounding jungle. Vai'shun had followed after her for a way, urging her to wait until daybreak, as the jungle at night was even more dangerous than in light, and she ought to have proper rest. But she explained, she only had four more days and nights to reach three other clans, and it was a very long way across the continent.

She paused long enough to remark, how very unusual it was, that the clans had traveled for centuries—so long that the story of the Boikk tree was deemed legend, ancient settlements had fallen to ruin, and the plants and animals had all but vanished— but remained so near the tree. They circled around and around, a twisted path, backtracking upon their own steps.

"After so many years of migrating, they should be a great distance away," Nej mused.

"And yet you traverse the same distance in a days time," Vai'shun remarked.

"And yet I do," Nej agreed.

"In four days then, Nej."

Nej nodded, and took leave once more.

She hadn't wished to admit it to Vai'shun, but she had another reason for leaving so hastily. While she now trusted Vai'shun, and believed he would protect her, and that it was unlikely any harm would come to her amongst the Koi'Tan, she had a lingering fear.

So many times she had been detained now, and finally having one of the fragments, she couldn't afford to lose it. Four days, and four fragments remained.

Somehow the jungle was easier to pass through this time. Nej suspected the fragment was an extremely powerful force. She felt guided along, simply knowing the way, and not a vine or flower or creature, not even tiny insects threatened her progress. She felt uncomfortable in the silence and stillness which surrounded her, but when she emerged from the jungle as the sun broke over the eastern horizon, she knew the fragment had been the key to her safe passage, and thought perhaps from now on, with the fragment and the tree on her side, her quest might become easier.

She paused a moment to consider her next course of action. Knowing Zuun was handling his peoples fragment in the east, Nej opted to return to her own people next as well. They would be the nearest, in so far as she could tell, as the Entari and Tayuuk had been moving farther north and east, while she had left her people in the western mountains, and they always traveled more slowly and cautiously than the other tribes.

It took her most of the day to cross from the southern jungle, over the grassland, around the great crater bearing the remains of the Boikk tree, and through the wasteland to the north which slowly became forest. Mountains rose up behind the trees, forming a ridge bearing east then south, blocking the Zenuran desert from view.

She crossed to the base of the mountains to the northeast, where the forest met the great slopes. Here there was a narrow stream trickling down the mountain, and Nej rested beside it, drinking from the cool water and scavenging a few berries from some scraggly bushes nearby. She ate more and more and soon closed her eyes, resting in the dappled shade of a spindly tree.

In the warmth of the afternoon sun, she didn't even notice as she drifted off...

With a gasp she sat up. Stars twinkled in the sky above and it was dark and cool. She felt refreshed, but she realized she had slept the rest of the day and well into the night. She hadn't noticed how exhausted she had become.

Scrambling to her feet, Nej observed her surroundings. Something seemed amiss. But all was quiet and still. It must have been her intuition that had roused her. Here it was, the second night, with only three remaining before the dawn when she must be back at the tree—practically where she was now.

How late was it? Likely the middle of the night, by how dark it was.

"*Sen va'lor*," she murmured, turning her hands as she spoke the incantation, and a glowing cobalt-hued light lifted from her hand and split into a cluster of tiny deep blue globes which twirled about, then spread around her, constantly darting this way and that, illuminating her path as she delved deeper into the forest. The glow was bright enough to see by, but dim enough not to attract attention, and being so small and glimmering, the orbs seemed more like moonlight filtering through trees. Moving with her, they did not reveal her form at all.

This forest, as Nej well knew, was mostly devoid of creatures; it held only tall old trees, thick bushes, and a dense layer of fallen foliage covering the ground. However, golems could be found everywhere, and they were her primary concern.

She made good progress through the woods and soon reached a rocky clearing. She stopped abruptly at the edge of the trees, scanning the open space before her suspiciously. Large boulders dotted the silent field, and the cool night wind stirred the long grasses, which brushed against the still forms. Nej took a cautious step forward, watching the stones warily.

Glow from the moon illuminated the meadow clearly. Her tread seemed noiseless, but an earth golem feels the slightest tremor in the ground, and when she reached the center of the field she froze as the sound of an avalanche erupted all around her; every massive stone unfurled itself and rose up into the form of an earth golem.

There was nowhere to run; she was surrounded by huge stone figures who began lunging and swinging at her. She dodged and rolled, around and through their legs, casting shields when she miscalculated and a limb came too near.

They closed in quickly. As the spaces between golems grew smaller, and her position tighter, she crouched down and cast a shield orb around herself. They began swinging at it, trying to break through the magic spell. Nej harnessed all the power she could, and then felt a pulse from her wrist; from the entity embedded there. With the extra energy she summoned a bright charged sphere, a glowing yellow-green ball of lightning-like energy, and thrust it against the ground, which sent a tremor rippling outward from her position. All the golems shook, wavered, and lost their balance, crumbling to the ground. Nej stood and the energy shimmered away from her. She lost no time; while the golems were trying to collect themselves, she raced past them to the northwestern end of the meadow and retreated into the safety of the trees.

Glancing at her covered wrist, Nej whispered, "Thank you," and was almost certain she felt a tiny pulse again.

As Nej delved deeper into the forest, she began to seek signs of her people. The forest was vast, dotted erratically with clearings, and the H'nomi had lived within it...forever, sometimes planting farms and building walls and lingering there in a village for a time, then when something would attack they would scatter and regroup at a new site.

When the earth golem and the Entari had attacked, they had been for several years living in a pleasant grove and managed to build up a supply of livestock. Though they always planned to reach the sea, they had instead remained within the forests, where it was safer, rather than crossing the open grasslands beyond.

Their current Chief had thought, perhaps from the highest mountain, Mount Hiito, they might see a new forest to escape to and move them further on their quest. Perhaps they could get a glimpse of the sea. Now Nej knew, there was no sea in sight.

Nej was uncertain which way they had gone, having spotted no indication of their presence, and considering it had been several days since she fled their camp.

She shuddered, recalling how she had been bound while under the effects of the Tayuuk magic. It made her frightened to return yet again to the H'nomi. How would they receive her this time?

Still she pressed onward, and at last saw flickers of firelight through the trees. A camp? As she neared, Nej discovered the camp did not resemble that of her people. Guttural sounds and large lumbering figures bespoke of the Tayuuk.

Taking a deep breath, Nej attempted to approach undetected as she searched for the large Chief's tent. For once her subterfuge was successful, and she was able to crawl through the brush and slip under the leather tent exterior where it met the forest undergrowth.

She realized this was a dangerous prospect as well; the Chief might attack first when an enemy unceremoniously appeared in his tent without permission.

Luck again was with her, as she found the Chief resting on some furs, eyes closed, undisturbed by her entry.

"Fier'lor," she said gently, maintaining her distance. His eyes flashed open, and he jerked his head to look at her. She watched the vivid glow emanating from his eyes soften as he recognized her. He rolled to his feet in a fluid motion, with unexpected agility given his massive size. Years of battle had trained his body for swift action.

He stepped toward her, looming ominously above, but she saw no malice in his visage as he eyed her curiously.

"You have returned. And something is different..."

He reached out and grasped her arm bearing the fragment.

"You have one!" He stripped the bracer from her wrist and gazed with interested at the glowing orb in her skin.

Nej looked away; the sight was not pleasing to her.

"I do, Sir. From the Koi'Tan. And I am seeking the remaining tribe leaders, in the hopes of obtaining their fragments as well."

She locked eyes with the Chief. "I must reunite the fragments and mend the tree. Our world is dying and it will only get worse unless we act now."

He chuckled, releasing her arm. "How did you acquire this? You kill the leader?"

"No, Sir. I was able to remove it without harming her. Though, without the fragments protection, she fell in battle shortly after I removed it."

He laughed again. "I do not fear death in battle. The fragment does not provide sufficient strength to outweigh my own prowess. However it does assure the allegiance of my tribe, and without it they may listen to no one."

"I believe you underestimate your authority, Sir."

"That may be. And for your sake I hope so."

There was a pause, and at last Nej asked, "Will you permit me?"

"Proceed."

Hesitantly, Nej lifted her left hand, moving it across Fier'lor's chest. The seed fragment in her wrist began to glow brightly as it passed over, and she saw a similar glow emanating from deep within his dark, thick, sinewy hide. Tayuuk were truly changed, she thought, on their exterior. But this one, at least, had a heart kinder than many, even of her own tribe.

She aligned her wrist over the fragment within Fier'lor and focused on drawing it out. He gave a yell of pain and she looked at him in surprise, quickly casting a healing spell in response, touching his skin with her right hand and allowing the energy to flow through.

He was different from the Koi'Tan leader. His fragment seemed embedded deeper; perhaps because he had born it longer, or because his physiology was unique.

"I'm sorry," she murmured, "It wasn't so bad last time."

Through gritted teeth Fier'lor growled, "Of course not—Koi'Tan are not Tayuuk."

Nej closed her eyes, putting all her power into the spell of healing, mending the fibers and tissue within as the slowly drew the fragment outward. She suspected it had been embedded within his very heart.

He roared and fell to his knees; Nej sank with him, feeling enormously guilty at the pain she was causing. She murmured an additional incantation and blue light emanated from her hand as well as the white healing threads; she was trying to dull the pain, to calm the nerves and allow the fragment to pass more easily through his tissue, which she repaired immediately behind.

His breathing steadied at this though his face still grimaced and she knew painful or not, it must be an unpleasant feeling to have something moving through your body of its own accord. Her hands began to shake and she began to feel dizzy from the focus and energy she used. At last the glow erupted through his skin and the fragment touched its equal in her wrist. Nej barely finished healing Fier'lor when she cried out in pain as her skin split for the fragments to join. Everything went dark as she collapsed into Fier'lor's arms.

He bandaged her wrist, then laid her on his furs to rest.

He took a moment to collect himself, sitting beside her with food and drink. It felt different to be without the fragment. But better. He was glad to be alone, on his own. He didn't envy Nej, bearing two fragments, and needing to collect more still—three more.

He saw how much energy it took from her to remove one from another. He wondered if she would be able to remove them from herself.

Nej slept for hours as Fier'lor watched on. At sunrise his

people were planning to break camp. Sunrise on the third day.

* * *

Nej awoke with a headache; the sun was shining brightly through the trees; the tent and camp had disappeared, all except for some furs beneath her, and a Tayuuk sitting near. He grunted.

"Awake at last," he muttered, rising to his feet.

"Come, let's catch the others."

She struggled to get to her feet, and he chuckled at her clumsiness. "You are fortunate I respect Fier'lor's will. He commanded I remain to look after you. Seems he was right—"

He broke off and suddenly gripped her arm with his large hand, steadying her before she fell. He continued, gazing at her inquisitively, "that you're in no condition to be left alone."

As he released her and bent to gather the furs he asked, "What happened to you?"

Nej smiled weakly, pleased by his consideration but uncertain if she should disclose the full details of her exploits to this Tayuuk. The Tayuuk, like the Koi'Tan, followed the idea that the one individual bearing the fragment ruled their clan. If she revealed that Fier'lor no longer held it, might the other Tayuuk turn on him? If she revealed that she, a weak H'nomi, bore not one but two seeds of power, would this Tayuuk turn on her?

"I have been on a very long journey," she offered, as they moved off following the steps the Tayuuk clan had left earlier.

"Over the mountains, across the desert, and through the jungle. I've even seen the remains of the ancient Boikk tree."

The Tayuuk said nothing, but his face was drawn and pensive.

"Have you not heard the tale?" Nej inquired.

He glanced at her.

"The tale of the Boikk tree?" she clarified.

With a wry grin, he said, "I haven't heard, no."

"Might I attempt to enlighten you as we walk?"

The Tayuuk extended a hand, palm upward, which she interpreted as inviting her to proceed.

"No one alive today remembers the Boikk tree, as it once was," she began. "It was generations ago, when it stood majestically over what was the Great Basin: a vast meadow filled with flowers, lush grasses, and countless animal species, all encircled by the wide Koing River.

"The tree provided for all. And all were safe and happy. Well, almost all were happy."

* * *

"You want to remake the tree, after they destroyed it once? What if someone destroys it again?"

They were striding at a fast pace, but Tayuuk on their own moved much quicker; she could tell her escort was traveling slowly to accommodate her. Having updated him briefly on the history of the tree, and how she wished to restore it, Nej found it intriguing that he posed the same concern everyone else, even she, had considered. Their conversation was cut short when they heard distant sounds of battle.

Nej looked to the hills in alarm; her new friend's eyes glowed maliciously and he broke into a run toward the noise. Nej suspected it was Tayuuk, but fighting who?

She hurried after him but he outpaced her by far. At last she stumbled upon the terrifying scene.

Tayuuk and H'nomi, but this time the H'nomi were not faring so well as when she had led them. Scanning the fighters, she saw Fier'lor, and her temporary guardian as well, tearing apart a H'nomi tent; she was about to go to Fier'lor and appeal to him to call off his people, when she caught sight of Jyu. He was struggling to block blows from a massive Tayuuk. Suddenly a green-tinged Tayuuk blade slashed down upon him. He tried to dodge, but the blade struck his leg deeply and he fell to the ground.

Nej screamed.

Her voice was so strong and so long that everyone ceased their action and looked at her. When at last she had their attention, she stopped, breathless.

"Why," she said at last, hoarsely.

"Why must you do this now."

She untied the bracer on her wrist and lifted her arm so all could see the glowing orbs there. The glow threaded down from her wrist to the ground, then branched out in all directions, touching each of them, as if an ethereal vine were twining amongst and holding them in place.

"There is a better way," she pleaded.

All gazed in wonder at her wrist. Fier'lor stepped through the stunned crowd toward her.

"Nej," he said, his voice gentle despite its natural gruffness, "My clan lives for the fight. When we crossed paths with your people, what could I say to stop them."

She looked to Fier'lor. "No explanation is needed. It is the way of our world to fight. But that is what I wish to change."

Nej addressed the remaining Tayuuk and H'nomi.

"Our people were once one clan: the H'toshen. We all lived peacefully, under the care of the great Boikk tree. A few elected to destroy our home; our way of life. And since, we've lived in war and fear, for so long that we are now on the verge of extinction.

"We are few," she insisted, and looking about themselves, the others new it to be true.

"In order for all our clans to survive, we must reunite. And plant a new tree, because not only are we destroying each other—the death of the tree destroyed the land and plant life around it. And that death is spreading.

"Help me save our world; help me save us all."

It may have been lucky for the strength of the fragments she bore, for they seemed to have a soothing quality, especially over the fiery Tayuuk. The Tayuuk backed off from the H'nomi, and H'nomi began to attend to their wounded.

Nej gazed into the crowd, her eyes finding Jyu once more. She raced to him; he was conscious, but looked pale, and was clutching his thigh and groaning. She gently examined the wound: a deep gash, with a sticky green substance filling, almost bubbling out of the incision, and a disturbing greenish-grey color spreading across his skin from the poison in his wound. Nej placed both hands over the injury and closed her eyes, allowing even the power of the fragments to mingle with her magic in an attempt to heal her friend.

His cries grew louder and she winced, hating to hear he was in pain. She heard footsteps behind her and a deep sigh.

"A friend of yours," Fier'lor remarked knowingly, and apologetically. "I am afraid our poison is magical, and spreads quite quickly. It is unlikely anything can be done," he explained.

Nej opened her eyes a moment, looking at Jyu; his leg was now darkening to black. Her eyes narrowed and she put all her energy into healing him. She could not lose him, as she lost Tiore. She murmured an incantation and deep blue light emanated from her hands; she called upon the tree, putting her wrist against his skin.

She cried out as her skin split, exposing the now combined pair of fragments. When they brushed his skin it seemed to light up, a bright glow shimmering across, and the color began to turn back to normal.

She drew the fragment directly across the wound and the poison hissed and shriveled and then disappeared, leaving only a thin line which continued to heal through her own magic.

But something wasn't quite right. On the outside, the skin had healed; but Jyu's face spoke of pain.

"It still troubles you?" Nej asked with concern.

He glanced at her sharply, perhaps unsure how to reply.

"The blade ran deep," Fier'lor spoke up again. He reached his massive hand down and prodded Jyu's leg with his fingers. Jyu grunted through gritted teeth. Fier'lor shook his head. "Our poison is magical," he repeated. "You may have saved his life, but deep within, the effect of the poison remains. In the bone, which does not mend so easily."

"What does it mean?" Jyu growled.

Fier'lor shook his head.

But Nej again held her hands over the wound. She let her magic flow through him, and she sensed that all was stabilized. Whatever pain lingered, she could not mend, for all was healed that could be.

"I am sorry, Jyu," she said softly. "You are healed as best I am able. It seems this magic has weakened you, causing continued pain. It should not spread further. But I know not how to do more."

Jyu seemed calmed by her words. He lifted his chin and his eyes narrowed in defiance. "If that's all, I can live with a little pain."

With determination, he forced himself to his feet again, then lifted a hand to help Nej up. She accepted, though she was still concerned for him.

"Thank you, Nej," he said solemnly. And he limped slowly away.

Nej felt anger rise within her. Her friend! He almost died, and for what. She gazed across the crowd until she spotted the H'nomi Chief. Then she stormed toward him, calling out to him as she neared.

"Chief!" He turned toward her questioningly, detecting the frustration in her voice. In her fury she struggled to find words. "Is it enough for you yet?"

"Nesjulin, what are you talking about," the Chief calmly replied.

"Don't you see? The time for fighting must end. Even your own son is injured, forever impacted by this foolish war.

"Let me end this. Let the suffering, the death, the sadness and fear disappear. When even the best are brought to the ground, it is clear the situation is beyond our control. Let us give the tree a chance."

The Chief wore a hardened expression, one of experience, pain, and time-earned wisdom.

"You think you know what is best for everyone," he countered slowly. "That the tree will cure all ills."

Nej held back her words, though she wished to contradict him.

"It will not. More will wish for and bring about its destruction again. And we will all be back where we began. The tree has been holding us back for centuries. How slowly we have marched. Yet, how easy it was for you, to return to the tree; how quickly you've traveled as you wished, because your desire was to restore the tree.

"Why have we moved away from it for centuries and yet traveled so small a distance? Why do we continue to walk on and on, and never reach our destination?

"Because the tree holds us back. And until it is completely dead, we will never be free. Your wish to restore it to health is exactly what it has been waiting for; hoping for. Sometimes, when all seems worst, you must press on—not turn back. When failure meets you at every step, it may not be that your path is wrong, but that your destination is so paramount that it requires great sacrifice, overcoming incredible challenge, and investing the highest faith and perseverance, to finally achieve."

The Chief paused, breathing heavily.

Nej considered his words. There was some validity in them after all. Still sure their division was a mistake, Nej asked at last, "How can peace be wrong?" And then, as if in a moment of clarity, she added, "Or perhaps, you are suggesting we should learn to get along and be peaceful without the presence of the tree?"

Nej felt uncertainty creeping into her heart, as she wondered if he could be right. Was there more to the legend that she didn't know? Was the tree sinister in some way? How could a peaceful, joyful life be bad? How could destroying a tree, that had never done any harm, be the right choice? She wished her lizard friend were here. Or Zuun. She needed time to consider. She wanted to do the right thing, and she wanted to feel confident enough in her decision to stand strongly behind it.

She heard other voices, cutting through her jumbled thoughts. She heard her people talking now, about the tree, the Tayuuk, and Jyu; she heard the Tayuuk gruffly arguing in their own language. She thought of the Koi'Tan, fighting over the fragment, over the power. She thought of Zuun, and wondered if he had been successful getting the fragment from his people, and what the result of meeting with the golems had been, or would be.

She thought of the decay. The ruin of the land around the tree. How nothing was growing, how the water was disappearing from the continent, how the animals had fled and were continually being pushed farther and farther away. How the animals supported the return of the tree. How only a giant, barren crater would remain, once the tree completely withered to nothing. How could this be right? How could death be better than life.

She turned to the Chief.

"Perhaps you fear losing your fragment; that death might overtake you. But I need the fragment now, to give back life to countless others. To guarantee the life of our people in the future. The tree may have been holding us back. But not for ill—for good. Because it knew that in order for us to survive, it must survive. All things wish to live, and all things have a right to live. It was wrong to destroy the tree, and it would be wrong not to help it now. The tree will only give life to the land. We are all still free to make our own choices, to travel where we wish, to live with whomever we prefer, to abide by our own rules and values, so long as we don't harm one another.

"Chief. Please let me use your fragment. I can't go on like this. Let me fix this world."

As the Chief stood motionless, the Tayuuk leader approached and agreed, "We have already given our fragment. We believe this is the right path as well. We cannot go on hunting forever; soon there will be nothing left to hunt."

"And the Koi'Tan also agreed that fighting is not the answer.

Chief, we H'nomi have always been against war. Surely you are not the only leader who desires it to continue."

The Chief argued bitterly, "Our wish was to leave this place! To see greater places beyond! To move apart from the mindless battles of the lesser clans. We are the only clan driven by our intellect, and renowned for it. Of course the other clans don't see what I see, they are not wise as the H'nomi. We will go far away, and leave them all in this barren wasteland they've created for themselves; leave them to destroy one another while we escape into a utopia beyond the seas!"

Shaking with anger, the Chief began to turn away, saying more calmly, "All those with me, let us go, and continue our journey; we will triumph over all others, when we at last reach our destination."

But as he walked slowly northward, no one moved. They saw the sadness on Nej's face, and felt as she did: that their leader had been corrupted, perhaps by the fragment, or by the degeneration that sometimes comes with the pursuit of an impossible dream. Most likely their endless journey had taken its toll, especially as he would be accountable if they failed, for it was his zealousness which lead them thus far.

The Tayuuk leader muttered to Nej, "Too much talk. I could strike him down now; you could get the fragment easily."

Nej sighed and shook her head at him. "Too much indeed but please, no."

The Chief had gone a few dozen paces when he realized he was alone and began to move slower, until he stopped entirely, head cast downward. Nej came up beside him and gently said, "You have a beautiful vision; a dream; a hope for us all. And your pride and courage have kept you fighting for that dream, no matter how little progress has been made; no matter who questioned your judgment.

"But how long should one keep fighting a futile battle? Sometimes there is more than one way to reach a goal. Sometimes the first way you try, is wrong, and you have to change your path.

"All of us see that this isn't working. There is no flaw in the desire to move beyond this land. But for centuries we've tried, to no avail. Let me help you achieve your goal. Perhaps by restoring the tree, you and those who share your vision can finally move beyond this continent.

"Please may I try."

The Chief didn't answer, but his face looked clear and thoughtful, his anger subsided. Nej turned to the others, with more excitement.

"We can all go, together. We can all travel back to the tree. Even some of the Koi'Tan may meet us there. We will share the results of this effort. You can see for yourself the effects of our ancestor's choice. And if my way doesn't work, we can work together to decide a new way, a better path, that will be mutually beneficial."

CHAPTER 12
Return to the Entari

Nej took a deep breath. Had she saved the most difficult for last? She had advised her people and the Tayuuk to make their way back to the tree; that she would meet them there in two days time. Jyu desired to join her on her last sojourn. He approached her as she was rebinding her wrist, covering the glowing, incomplete seed with a length of multicolored cloth.

"I'll come with you," Jyu offered. "My bow will be useful, and you may need protection. The Entari as a whole aren't so cruel, but their leader is vicious; heartless. She'll be the real challenge, and you might need a hand if debates go badly."

"Jyu...thank you," Nej began, "But please, this has been my task all along. I am grateful for your aid with the Tayuuk and our own clan; you've been unbelievably supportive. But let us not risk you in this. See these fragments I now carry? I believe they make me stronger; safer. I believe the Entari will not be able to harm me. Of course I could be wrong, but I am hoping that what is right and good will triumph, and I believe I am on that side."

"You really ought to have someone with you Nej. Look at how difficult it has been each time. Two is better than one."

"I have a friend amongst the Entari. Perhaps a few, as I was their resident healer for a time," she smiled ruefully. "Please help our people reach the tree and maintain their courage. And perhaps you'll have some idea how we can mend the tree. Because even though I have these fragments, I may need additional assistance in executing my plan. Furthermore, Jyu—there will be golems coming."

"What!"

"The area around the dead tree is an empty crater; the land is cracked and sinking. It needs to be filled, with water and dirt, before we plant the new tree. I've met a Zenuran with a friendly golem, who is going to try to gain the confidence of some hostile golems, then convince them to join us and create the needed elements. But I cannot guarantee what will happen when they find all the clans there. Will they remain peaceful; will his golem be able to control them, and protect all of you."

"I see," Jyu said solemnly. "Very well; in the event that the golems arrive before you do, and there is any difficulty; or should another clan behave...unexpectedly, I will stay with our people."

"Thank you Jyu," Nej said, and wrapped her right arm around him, giving him a tight hug. With a smile, she turned and hurried off to the northeast.

She followed the route she had taken before, when she met the Entari camp below the cliff where the Tayuuk had been resting. From there she tried to scout, to track footprints across the grassy plains. It was fairly easy to do. The soldiers were not careful, trudging heavily across the brittle grasses.

They had moved far, Nej thought, as she continued moving northward. She had been tracking for hours now. Of course the last time she saw the Entari was several days prior. If they had continued moving all that time, it might take her days to find them.

She recalled how the tribes typically seemed to circle around and around, and even though they walked for days, years, centuries, they continued to travel the same paths, always having to backtrack due to enemies, or to find water or food. Now, because she had deterred the Tayuuk from attacking the Entari army, the Entari had been free to move unchallenged. Perhaps for once, they had finally gotten beyond the range of the ever-weakening Boikk tree. Perhaps they had found the mysterious sea and were finally gone from the lands forever. Maybe she was wrong, and there *was* more, and this one tree meant nothing to the rest of the world.

The plains seemed to go on forever. The sun had dipped below the mountains and Nej found her eyes struggling to see in the twilight. She conjured a small light in her palm and held it in front of her. It wasn't much, but it prevented her from tripping over the tall grasses. They were growing taller now, she thought. And the ground seemed moist and muddy. Her feet stuck as she walked. Branches and vines jutted sporadically from the ground and she had to step more carefully.

Not a creature in...

A loud sound struck her and her eyes grew wide, looking to the sky. A shriek, the call of a bird, echoed across the empty air. There were few animals on the lands anymore. Only in the southern jungles; some in the forested mountains. But these dry plains were habitable only by hardy creatures—reptiles, insects, and very small mammals. Birds couldn't stay, as there were no trees or shelter. She was farther north than she had ever been. And yet the Entari had come this way, she was certain. She still saw imprints here and there from their boots, and broken grass from their passing.

In the encroaching darkness, Nej could detect only an immense, indistinct mass ahead, stretching as far as she could see in either direction. Scrubs laced the tall grass; bushes, heavy vines, and thick roots slowed her progress. She began to pass large trees, and now the ground was wet indeed. She stepped onto the tough vines erupting from the ground and hopped across from root to vine to stone, avoiding the swamp water all around. Sounds were everywhere, imposing; confining. This place was truly alive. Water creatures, insects, calls of night birds, hissing and slithering sounds in the water and muck. And now, all was dark, so dark she could barely see her skin, and her glowing orb seemed too bright to her eyes. She sent it off a bit further in front of her.

As creatures scurried by, she would get a glimpse of soft fur or shiny scales. Glints of talons and beaks would flash in the air when birds swept down upon prey. Everything seemed large here; plants, trees, vines, animals. As if she was in a prehistoric place, wild and dangerous. It was much like the southern jungles, but this was a cool swamp, murky and dark and menacing—and not only because it was night.

She thought she saw flickers of light, very far in the distance, through the trees and vines. She thought maybe she heard voices amid the nocturnal noises.

Suddenly there was a very loud rushing sound and a great hiss as a huge snake emerged from the ever-deepening swamp water. Glittering fangs flashed and struck at her; she barely dodged the wide head and splashed into the water as she tripped on the gnarled roots of the tree she had been standing on.

She struggled to climb back on; she didn't like the water and didn't want to stay in for fear of what else lurked beneath the surface. Already she felt as though things were clinging to her, dragging her down. She was almost grateful for the darkness so she couldn't see what they might be. The snake was rushing again, striking at her; she ducked below the roots, pulling herself around the tree from the underside, thrashing roughly against the grasping water weeds.

The snake suddenly disappeared; she heard the gentle sound of water moving as it dove under. She managed to pull herself back onto the roots, but found she was trapped there. She cast her light about her, surveying the terrain. The swamp water had become deep and the trees were farther apart now. She would have to swim some distance to reach the far north edge, where there was an area of muddy ground again. And possibly, this snake could travel on ground as well as in water.

She heard rippling in the water and looked frantically about for an escape. She noticed a low branch on the tree and jumped for it, pulling herself up, pushing against the trunk of the tree, until she was perched atop. Then she looked for more branches to draw herself higher up into the tree.

As she reached up and grabbed an overhead limb, there was a shrill "Squawk!!" and something pierced her hand.

Nej gave an exclamation of pain and withdrew her hand involuntarily, then lost all grip and fell hard upon some lower branches. Feathers were fluttering all around her and she covered her face with one arm, trying to crawl away amid beaks, talons, and wings. She fumbled to the far side of the tree and inched outward along a branch, the birds pursuing her relentlessly.

When she was clear of the tree's roots she dropped down into the water, escaping the birds. As water 'things' began to grasp at her again, she splashed and swam frantically for shore. Finally her feet felt sticky mud below them and she crawled, panting, onto the embankment. She lay a moment, exhausted, barely beyond the water's edge. Then she heard sounds from in front of her. She tried to lift herself up but all her limbs felt weak and helpless.

Footsteps drew near and torches became visible in the

darkness. At first she was relieved; it must be Entari. But then she thought, if Korr was not among this search party they may not recognize her; they might kill her. She knew the Entari killed on sight, much like the Tayuuk. She never asked Korr why he hadn't.

"Here!" a voice shouted, and she saw the glint of a silvery blade in the firelight. Soldiers surrounded her and she felt the cold, sharp metal touch her skin as the voice darkly said, "Who are you."

Suddenly a splash of water erupted behind her as the snake emerged from the depths! There were scrapes of metal as the Entari scouting party drew their weapons and turned their attention on the beast instead of her.

Someone pulled her away from the fight, dragging her clear of danger. She tried to gather her strength, pushing herself up off the ground. She met Korr's eyes, then closed hers, letting out a breath of relief.

He lifted her to her feet and supported her at the waist, leading her toward the glimmering firelight of the Entari camp. She could hear the battle was faring well; soon the sounds of fighting ceased and only the sheathing of weapons and slow footfalls followed them to the Entari camp.

Korr brought her directly into his tent, and found some drink and a bite to eat. While she tried to partake of this, he observed her and playfully remarked, "You're a terrible scout, you know that."

She almost choked on her drink as she laughed, then admitted, "...I know."

"But I got to you unseen once!"

"*Once*," he repeated with emphasis. Then added, "So why did you leave? And why have you come back? You rarely drop by for a mere social call."

Nej nodded in agreement. "I have been traveling these many days since I last saw you. I have been seeking the tribal leaders to collect these—"

Korr gaped as she unwound the binding on her wrist and displayed the tiny glowing orb; the three seeds had fused into one and their roots seemed to be spreading further across her skin. It scared her. But she had to transport them—and finish her task.

"There are five fragments in all; together they gave life to the great Boikk tree, centuries ago, before our people destroyed it. I have sought you out because I must request permission to take the Entari fragment back to the place where the tree lies dying, and reunite the fragments to heal the tree."

Korr was distracted by the appearance of her wrist with the vivid orb affixed.

"Can you remove that?" he asked, uncomfortably.

"I believe so," Nej replied, hastily wrapping the cloth around her forearm again. "I removed each fragment from the other clan leaders, through my magic, and I believe I can do it again. So far it is the only way I know to safely take them from a living creature. You see they are quite drawn to life."

He took a deep breath and shook his head.

"Well I haven't seen anything like that before. But Myra would be the one to ask."

"I have not yet found favor in Myra," Nej admitted. "Perhaps it will not be so this time."

Nej paused and added, "Your people have come far, these past days. It was difficult and time-consuming to reach you."

"I have lost track of how many suns fell since you disappeared from our number," Korr agreed. Nej glanced away guiltily. "But we have moved quickly as we were unhindered. Not a golem or Tayuuk, not anyone to fight until now—a few beasts in this swamp."

"What do you think lies beyond?"

"We never do know. This is the farthest we've come."

Nej sat lost in thought. The words of the H'nomi Chief still echoed in her mind, and she wondered if perhaps there was more out there, and if the tree was truly hindering them from finding it. Was it better to live in peace and happiness, but ignorant and isolated? And what was to prevent them from traveling beyond these lands after the tree was healed? Surely it could not cause them any harm to mend what they had broken.

"Well, if I may have the fragment, I will leave you to continue in your desired course. I am curious how far you might get. And I would certainly seek you out after my task is complete, and see what wonders you've discovered."

Korr smiled momentarily at this, before a look of concern crossed his face. He seemed to struggle for words, then gave up and instead offered lightly, "I'll take you to Myra now if you like."

Though she wondered what Korr had been thinking, Nej merely nodded.

Korr escorted Nej out, through the camp, and to the Commander's tent. It was late into the night and most of the soldiers were sleeping. A few stood at guard around the perimeter. The Commander's tent had a great many weapons before it, and extra wooden barricades around its stiff leather walls. A light still glowed from within.

Korr gave a nod to the man standing outside, then tapped on the tent flap, softly calling, "Commander, it's Korr. Might I have a word?"

A muffled voice was heard from inside. Nej, standing somewhat back, couldn't distinguish the answer, but Korr glanced at her meaningfully, then pushed aside the flap and drew Nej inside.

Myra turned as they entered, saying "What is it?" cutting off abruptly when she caught sight of Nej.

"I see," Myra said coolly.

Korr lifted a hand, saying, "No, no—it's not as you think. Nej has come to speak with you. She has a…request. If you have a moment."

Myra lifted an eyebrow. "Fine," she muttered at last, indifferently. As if to reaffirm her apathy, she turned back and began gathering items from a wood table and stowing them in a bag. Nej stepped forward.

"Commander," she said politely, "I have sought you out once more, because I am in great need of your help.

"As you likely know, long ago, our clans were one. And we all lived in peace under the care of a great tree. That tree lies dying now, and the land around it continues to decay in a spreading blight. Eventually our entire continent may be engulfed, perhaps before we can reach the coveted sea.

"Please help me to restore the great tree, and the lands around it. Give those who wish to stay here a chance to live in peace, before the rest travel away, perhaps forever, to seek their glory. All I need is your fragment, to complete the seed and give the tree new life."

Myra stood still for a time. Then at last she faced Nej. As with many of the other leaders, suspicion and disapproval played on her face.

"You need just my fragment?" Myra pressed.

"Only yours, now that I have all the others," Nej corrected. Myra's brow furrowed.

"Really? How could you achieve that—they all agreed with you?"

"Yes, Commander; everyone has agreed to meet at the site of the tree, and attempt to restore it, and in doing so restore health and beauty to the surrounding landscape. Even the golems will come, to aid us in our endeavor."

"The golems!" Myra said in disbelief. "This is extraordinary. So if I were not to comply I would be the only one standing against? I cannot believe the Tayuuk even...and you have met the Koi'Tan?" Myra's voice trailed off and she began to pace her tent while she mused.

"I would never give you the fragment," she remarked, "if it were not that all others had already done so." Spinning back to Nej she said sharply, "Have you any proof of what you say? Where are the fragments now?" Nej gulped, then gently untied the cloth covering her wrist. She slowly extended her arm and Myra rushed forward, her eyes wide as she gazed with wonder at the glowing orb embedded in her skin.

"They are fused together," Nej started to explain, but Myra nodded her head.

"I see, I see." Myra's interest was keen.

"Let us go at once," she said abruptly.

"Korr, gather the troops, we will all return to the tree."

She looked back to Nej with a tight smile. "I will be your escort."

Nej wasn't sure how this change had come about. Myra's unusual support made Nej uneasy, but she tried to think positively. Perhaps the strength the fragments supposedly provided caused Myra to show her more respect.

Korr awoke the clan members and informed them of the change of plan. Myra had Nej assist her in packing and tearing down her own tent. In short order, the entire camp was deconstructed and ready to move.

They fought some snakes and predatory birds as they retraced their steps southward, but had no trouble defeating them, and soon escaped the swamp. They proceeded southwest, moving across the dry plains quickly, trying to make up for the time Nej had lost in traveling so far to reach them.

Korr was perturbed by Myra's newfound interest in Nej. The

two women were inseparable. He kept a close eye on both.

"When are they all to meet?" Myra would ask time and again, then study her map and glance at the position of the sun.

"I believe we can make it in time."

Nej was relieved, and yet increasingly discomforted by Myra's enthusiasm. She felt perhaps Myra was hiding something—a deeper, darker agenda. It didn't fit her nature to be so generous. Nej wished to discuss her fears with Korr, but Myra never gave her a chance, keeping her close at all times.

They traveled the rest of the night and the next very long day, with only brief breaks to eat and drink, until darkness settled firmly and stars shone bright across the sky. Nej hadn't slept soundly in two days, but in the next morning they must meet the others.

They were high into the forested mountains now, and Nej thought they must be only a few more hours from the tree. They could easily pass the night here and rise at dawn to meet the others. But Myra seemed oblivious to Nej's well-being, which, Nej thought, was normal, and contradictory to her pretense of caring about Nej's ultimate goal. Korr however, did care for Nej, and at last approached her despite Myra's presence.

"Nej, you don't look well. Perhaps we should stop and rest," he remarked loudly, directing his words toward Myra.

Myra turned, surprised. "Oh…yes, I suppose so." She studied the sky and looked habitually at the map in her hands. "Yes, even with a few hours pause, we should be able to reach the tree," she admitted.

Closing the map and looking up, she fished for an explanation. "It would be best to reach the tree before the others, but I suppose if we must be the last to arrive, it cannot be helped. I will study our route. At least, if the golems are all at the tree, we should not have any battles slowing our progress." Myra turned sharply and strode off, leaving Korr and Nej alone at last.

Korr escorted Nej to a soft, mossy spot beneath a tree. He began to lay out some cloth for a bed and enticed her to rest.

"Korr," she said, as she sat next to him, "I don't trust Myra. I am grateful she agreed to come, but she has not yet given me the fragment."

Korr pondered this. "She has been keeping you under an excessively tight watch," he agreed. "I don't know her intentions. But we needn't trouble ourselves over what goes on in her mind;

we could theorize all day and fail to uncover the truth. Instead I will stay near you, and be ever vigilant.

"Besides," he added lightly, "With so many fragments in you, it isn't likely any harm could befall you. I am certain Myra will pass the fragment when we reach the tree and she sees that all you have said is true."

Nej wasn't so sure, but she smiled anyway, knowing he was trying to ease her mind. She fell asleep quickly beside Korr, who kept his word and stayed near, despite others' attempts to draw him away.

CHAPTER 13
Golems

Vierux and Zuun too had reached the treeline, and were approaching the base of the mountains, but much farther to the south. Desert sands swirled about them as they raced into the shelter of the forest. It had taken them two days to design and construct a portable container for the seed, one containing ample water and dirt to keep it growing, surrounded by a sturdy casing that would protect it from harm. It took so long particularly because Vierux had other matters to attend to much of the time.

This special box Vierux placed in a shoulder bag, along with some supplies for their journey. They had waited one more night and began their trek on the morning of the third day; the same morning Nej encountered the H'nomi, and then traveled on in search of the Entari.

Vierux remarked that she wondered if it was not childish of her to leave a "note" for her guards explaining where she had gone and what they intended to do. Like a young girl running away from home, afraid to tell her parents face to face for fear of their negative reaction. Zuun laughed. "That's alright, at least we're on our way without further complication. Maybe they'll come after you as you requested, to join the other clans at the tree."

Their first step, of course, was befriending some golems. Zuun and Jett agreed that earth golems, like Jett, would be the most understanding and sympathetic to their cause. Though they could be fierce when enraged, and wouldn't stop until their vengeance had been sated, they also had greater attunement with nature and living things. Plants often grew on them, much to their pleasure. They might be willing to restore the tree. And their dirt was needed most, to fill the voids wrenched by the dying arbor.

Near the eastern base of the mountain range, at the edge of the desert, they took a break, a meal and a siesta, and then began their search for earth golems. Of course they had a good idea where to look; earth, air, and fire golems all frequented the desert, but earth tended to stay where larger areas of rock prevailed.

They spent the afternoon weaving through the somewhat sparse woodland, climbing along the mountain edge, moving southward. Zuun was about to suggest they split up, one going south and the other north, when Vieroux announced, "There!"

Pointing up the mountain, there seemed a shallow cave, sheltered by some trees and bushes. Rocky creatures occasionally stepped into view then disappeared deeper into the inlet.

"Let's go," Zuun decided.

The trio had yet to cross barren mountainside to reach the cave; as they neared the camp they feared the golems would detect them prematurely, but they managed to gain the cover of the foliage before any of the clan took notice, from where they rested in the wide cavern cut into the mountain face.

They crouched inside a large, thick-leafed bush; Jett waited behind a wide tree.

"We should send Jett," Zuun whispered. "They won't attack him. But we'll be here in case they...do."

Vieroux nodded, serene but notably uneasy.

Zuun slid nearer to Jett. "You ready for this?"

Jett whirred slightly and said in his quietest voice, "I am, Zuun." Zuun nodded to him, and with a sigh, assured, "We'll be right here, watching. We'll join you if you signal, or if it seems like you need help." With a weak smile, he set Jett off with a pat on the leg, ducking deeper within the bush again as Jett stepped out into the open and approached the golems.

"Greetings, friends," he called robotically.

The golems all turned, immediately on alert, gunned arms raised and leveled, battle-ready. Jett wisely stopped moving, putting his robo-hands up before him. "Ahh, be at peace friends, as you can see I am an earth golem like you."

He slowly began stepping nearer, lowering his hands as he spoke. "I was damaged when my companions took on a group of fire golems. I fled, tumbled down the mountain, and though I was able to repair myself, I have since been separated from golem-kind."

The golems had lowered their weapons. One now approached Jett and brought him into their circle. "A rough patch you have been through," he said. "Join us, and stay among our number as long as you like."

So much so good. Zuun had crept back beside Vierux. She softly whispered, "So they have accepted him. But how will he get out of his lie?"

Zuun just shook his head, hoping his friend had a plan.

As night began to fall, the golems began to close their eyes and shut down. Zuun saw Jett flash a tiny light in his direction, unnoticed by any others. Zuun nudged Vierux. "He has signaled us. Let us watch closely now for our moment of entrance."

Suddenly Jett, in an angry voice, shouted, "Hey, that's mine!" And his blade arm lifted up and crashed down upon one of the other golems. The sleeping golems stirred, drawn to the shouts and clashing metal, as Jett and more golems started yelling and fighting.

"What's going on here!"

"He has stolen my gems! Just look!"

"I have not, I don't know how they got here, it wasn't—AHHH!"

Jett was slashing and thrashing every which way, and the golems didn't know what to do; some were defending themselves while they tried to subdue him, others backing off uncertainly. Jett focused on the one golem, pushing it back toward where Zuun and Vierux waited. He knocked the golem down and rose his arm to deliver what would certainly be a finishing blow, when Zuun leapt from his hiding place, swung atop Jett's shoulders and quickly flipped some switches on the back of his neck. Jett slowly lowered his arm, calm and docile again.

The earth golems approached, as Zuun hopped down from Jett and began attending the damaged golem, repairing him perhaps faster than the golems could have.

"What is this!" One golem roared, pointing a blade toward Zuun. Zuun turned and looked at him, while the golem he'd been fixing sat up, impressed with the adjustments already made, his artificial mind assessing what had transpired and what damage he had sustained.

Zuun felt it best to say nothing and let his actions speak for themselves.

"He has saved me," the downed golem said, somewhat incredulous. Zuun rose, and put out a hand to help the golem up. The golem took it.

"Sorry," said Zuun, "I didn't mean to intrude. My friend and I were passing through these woods on our way to the Boikk tree. I heard the uproar and came to see what the trouble was."

He paused, taking a little breath.

"I am from the Zenura tribe. I'm familiar with golem construction," he explained. "I know an enraged golem when I see it. He wasn't acting how my forefathers intended at all. So unfortunate, that you golems share the same mood swings as us organics." He tried to smile, then glanced nervously around.

"Er—may I go?" he asked at last, gesturing away from the cove.

The golems were intrigued however, and invited him to come into their camp. "And bring your...friend," they added. Vierux rose slowly from the brush and stepped forward. The golems were enchanted.

They spoke at length about the creation of the golems, and their emotions and other characteristics that seemed more organic than mechanical.

"We have long fought your people, our makers," the leader of the group said at last, "But perhaps there is room for understanding. You seem to recognize us as individuals; as learning, growing, feeling beings. Not robotic slaves with no desires of our own."

"That's right," Zuun agreed. "You are much more than the first creator believed, or anticipated. And that can be no mistake. You are wonderful assets to our people and our world. If only we could put our differences and history aside, and move forward together."

Vierux smiled at him and nodded in agreement.

Zuun looked around at the other golems, who gazed back attentively. He looked as though he was in deep contemplation. Suddenly he looked right at the leader, as if an idea had burst into his mind, and asked, "Will you help us?"

"Help you? How?"

"See, we're traveling to the Boikk tree," Zuun began, "Or

rather, what remains of it. We wish to reunite all the clans at the tree. Morning after tomorrow, actually.

"We plan to grow a new tree. Trouble is, the land around the old tree is destroyed and withering away. How can we plant a tree where there is no earth? But, if *you* could help us..." his voice trailed off, as if the idea were still forming in his mind. His hint was clear enough to the golems, who knew their own capabilities.

"Yes," one said. "Yes, we could heal earth for you."

Another quietly spoke up, "And if we could find some water golems, and convince them—"

"They would never align with us!"

"Perhaps they will, once they know all the organic clans are attempting to make amends. Perhaps it is time for us too."

* * *

They spent the remainder of the night with the golems, sleeping in the shallow cave. At first morning light the pair, in company with the small band of golems, moved south along the mountain, then westward again, up and over the low plateau Zuun and Nej had traversed a few days prior. On their way down, the golems mentioned there was a stream a bit northward, where they may be likely to find some water golems.

They shifted their path, following the mountain northward to where water trickled down the western face. This they traced, until Vierux suddenly put out a hand to stop them. She pointed below, and through the trees they could see, immersed in the narrow stream, numerous water golems.

Still being some distance up the mountain, the earth golems blended in nicely with rocky surroundings and hadn't been seen by the water golems below. Gathering together, the golems and Zenura discussed.

The golem band leader asked, "How can we approach them peacefully?"

Jett stepped forward. "I could stage a diversion," he offered. "We know my aggressive tendencies," he stole a wink to Zuun.

"No," insisted the leader. "Once these golems become angered, we may not be able to quell them. We must gain their trust immediately."

"May I try," asked Vierux. Zuun looked at her in surprise.

The golems shifted about indecisively.

"I have a way with water," Vierux coaxed. "And I have an idea."

"Water golems are highly volatile," Zuun warned. "I don't recommend approaching so many on your own."

"I will be quite alright and cause no harm to any golems," she assured.

"Proceed," the earth golem leader agreed, having little other option. Vierux nodded, then skirted stealthily down the hillside, moving effortlessly amongst rocks and trees, staying hidden from the golems gracing the stream.

She reached the base of the mountain, and there took from her bag a small container. She opened it, and began speaking softly. She moved forward, closer and closer to the golems. At last one saw her, and started to give a cry, but then noticed how calmly she moved, slowly and gently like water itself. He saw too that she was alone, and posed no threat to the many water golems there.

Other golems saw her now too, and began to approach. She reached the stream, and the nearest golem. The others drew in around her, encircling her.

She gave a faint smile, then returned to a pensive expression, attempting to ease her nervousness.

"Would it help," she said quietly, "if the water were a fountain?" She had noticed they were drinking and bathing, but the stream was very shallow, drying up like the surrounding environment, and the golems were having a difficult time enjoying the water. The golems said nothing; as there was no opposition, Vierux proceeded.

Kneeling down, she extracted the fragment and lowered it into the water. Holding it loosely, yet securely, she closed her eyes. Shimmering blue energy washed over her, spinning around her hands and the fragment, being drawn into it, rushing faster and brighter until water flew up through her hands, erupting out of the fragment and into the air, then raining down upon the golems below, who seemed to smile in delight, raising their arms to the welcome shower.

When they had enjoyed the water for some time, Vierux lowered the fountain until it was a mere trickle, and eventually the water disappeared entirely from her hands and the fragment.

Suppressing a shudder at having touched the life form again, she hastily returned the fragment to its container and placed it in her bag.

The golems gathered around her, pleased.

"Thank you," said the first one who'd seen her. "It was kind of you to share that with us. We've never seen anything like it." She smiled. "My pleasure. And thank you for allowing me to approach you. And if I may, I have a favor to ask of you."

"Ask," the golem permitted.

"I am the leader of the Zenura. I am taking my fragment from the destroyed Boikk tree back to its roots. Members from all five clans are meeting tomorrow to reunite the five fragments we stole, and restore the lands to health and abundance. I have with me, some earth golems, to help in the restoration of the soil. Will you join us, and aid in restoration of water?

"For that magic you have just seen," she continued, "Could not have been possible without your powers as well. I channeled your water energy to create the fountain. And with your help, and the full power of the joined fragments, we may be able to create a permanent water source that will feed the continent indefinitely."

The golems murmured amongst one another, their voices like the rush of water in a rocky river: rapids and falls, splashing and churning.

"Yes," said the first golem at last. "Yes we would like this. Our waters have grown stagnant and small. We are thirsty, and we know our end is near. If the earth golems are ready to work together, then we too will come to your aid."

With a wide smile Vierux motioned, and Zuun and the earth golems emerged from the wood, as they had continued slowly down the mountainside unnoticed while Vierux had created her display. The golems greeted one another, and Zuun approached Vierux.

"I didn't know you could do that! We don't even need the golems if you can create water."

"I can't do it alone. As you can see, there is water here, and water golems. I can use water, or the golems, to generate more water. Coupled with the power of the fragment of course. You see, as you build earth golems, my specialty is water golems."

Zuun smiled. "Why you had this in a fountain," he tapped the bag at her side.

They opted to spend the remainder of the day seeking more golems, with similar success in joining them to their cause, then enjoyed a remarkably pleasant evening, talking, laughing, dancing, even sparring, late into the night. Zuun mostly observed from a distance, silently making notes on what had happened, having a great deal of hope for the future, seeing how it was possible for enemies to become friends.

CHAPTER 14
United We Stand

The clans, and golems, were beginning to arrive at the site of the Boikk tree.

Incidentally, the Koi'Tan were the first to appear, from the south. When they reached the edge of the decaying region, they slowed their approach, spreading out and surveying the area with great interest, taking everything in. As they neared the center, the site where the great tree once stood, they could see figures beyond, to the north—the H'nomi, with the massive Tayuuk.

Once all three clans had amassed near the tree, greeting one another at long last, they saw movement from the east: Golems marching out of the forested mountain base. Some became alarmed, but the leaders reminded them that the Zenura planned to bring some golems to aid in replenishing the land. This did not entirely assuage their uncertainty, considering the large number of golems and their malignant history. Several individuals kept weapons at the ready. Only the Koi'Tan did not recognize the golems as foes, having been hidden away in their jungle, spared from any interaction with the great constructs.

It wasn't until the golems, with just two Zenura, came quite near that the Entari at last peeked over the mountains to the northeast.

Unseen to the tribes below, the Entari began to prepare for their descent. Myra called for a halt and ordered everyone to gather around.

"Now is our chance," she announced, in her most authoritative voice, eyes piercing and violent. "All our enemies lie below us, unsuspecting of any attack. They come believing we will all live in peace now; all give up our ways: our strength, our courage, our bravery, our skill from years of training! I will not give up my sword, nor will I cease my quest for honor and glory! Now is our chance to conquer these lands, before moving on to even greater challenges beyond!"

Nej paled during this revelation and backed slowly away, shrinking into the shadows. She looked nervously between the faces of the Entari, searching for signs of their intent. She backed into someone and gasped, spinning around; it was only Korr.

She stared silently at him, terrified he might support Myra in her plot. But his face told otherwise. He looked disappointed; concerned, and he shook his head gently.

"Her idea is mad," he whispered, and they both looked back at Myra, who was still raving to the others. "They must see it. Even if we would wish to continue our ways, attacking here, now, will bring us nothing but death. It would have been better if we never returned—if I alone had escorted you back with the fragment."

Nej forced a smile. "Thank you Korr," she said softly, "For being on the side of peace and understanding."

Korr almost chuckled. "It isn't peace or understanding, it's logic. Did you see those golems? All the Tayuuk? And the Koi'Tan? They're fierce fighters, and would never be overtaken. We are outnumbered at least four to one. All the others have amassed peacefully and will work together if attacked. We cannot win."

Nej smiled for real this time. This was a true Entari speaking.

Then they heard Myra calling for Nej. Korr and Nej crouched down within the brush as Myra began to reveal her darker plan, which Nej had secretly feared. They would take the fragments from Nej and combine them in Myra, who would then be unstoppable and destroy everyone. Even Korr conceded that with the strength of all the fragments, she could possibly defeat the others and have power over them. Nej admitted that it was not *all* the fragments she possessed; there was one fragment still unrecovered. Korr frowned.

"Myra won't believe you," he whispered. "Likely she won't even care—she may deem four fragments sufficient. That's how twisted her mind has become in this quest for power."

Suddenly Myra looked around. "Find Nej, and bring her to me. We will need the fragments she carries to combine them and make me the strongest force on this continent."

Nej again looked fearfully to Korr. Would he protect her? Korr immediately rose and stepped boldly out of the trees. Some of the others were roving about, searching for Nej; most stood in groups, discussing the development in hushed voices. But none wished to speak against Myra. They knew she was the strongest of them all; even stronger than she appeared.

"This plan defies logic," Korr said loudly, for all to hear. His comrades slowly stopped what they were doing and faced him. "We are vastly outnumbered. We might be able to defeat just one clan single-handedly, though we have never done it before. Now we have three full clans and dozens of golems before us! And they all came prepared for battle, despite the prospect of peace, because they are meeting clans they've mistrusted for generations.

"Myra," Korr directed his words to her now, and she looked back, perhaps less irritated by his apparent treachery than he expected, which he found more unnerving. "We will not win this battle. Even with the strength of the combined fragments, it is only *you* who will have immunity from death, while your entire army will fall around you."

Myra's face hardened, and all the others looked to her questioningly. Voices began to murmur throughout their numbers again. Was she driven mad by want of power? Was her greed so extreme she would sacrifice all of them to achieve it? And what of this Nej, who currently carried so many fragments, yet desired to use their power for the good of all. She who had healed many of them in the past, even though they now knew she was supposedly an enemy. Perhaps these other clans were not their enemy either; perhaps their leader had mislead them.

A queer smile toyed on Myra's face. "It was you, Korr, who brought Nej to us. So perhaps I have you to thank for this opportunity. But your refusal to comply with my commands suggests you've been on her side all along."

"Myra, don't make unfounded assumptions—" Korr retorted in annoyance.

"I am the leader of the Entari!" Myra shouted indignantly. "And I demand allegiance from all my soldiers!" She glared at Korr icily. "*When* we take over the tribes below, *you* will be the first to go."

Korr's eyes narrowed and he drew his sword. "And I will defend myself," he said quietly, but resolutely. None of the others moved, against Korr or Myra. They seemed uncertain who was right. Korr's judgment was sound, but Myra was their leader.

At last Korr announced, "I declare Myra unfit to lead us! I challenge her command, and demand a duel, here, now. May the winner have the trust, respect, and allegiance of all Entari!"

A myriad of gasps, cheers, and shouts erupted from the soldiers. Myra, seething with rage, drew her own blade, and stepped forward.

"I meet your challenge, Korr," she hissed. Then she smiled evilly and raised her sword.

As metal clashed, over and over, Nej winced in the shadows, wondering if Korr would be able to overpower Myra in spite of the fragment she bore. She remembered all Tiore had said.

She watched Myra slowly but surely push him back, clearly having the upper hand.

She knew she would have to act if Korr were to win. She had fragments too, and their power could help him. She focused on the fragments, channeling their energy, pulsing it toward Korr. The fragments glowed brightly on her arm, even showing through the fabric and it was painful; the fragments sensed the presence of Myra's piece and wished to draw together. But Nej's combined fragments were stronger, and Myra felt herself become distracted, losing focus, as her fragment tried to pull away from her.

It was enough for Korr to repel Myra, landing heavy strikes over and over until Myra was near the edge of the mountain and at last disarmed. Korr, holding his blade against Myra, said, "You are defeated, Myra. Relinquish command to me." The others gazed on expectantly, knowing Korr was their rightful leader now. But would Myra accept it? Entari dislike losing power, and most would rather die than accept the humiliation of a lesser position.

"You're blind, Korr," she growled. "Giving up all that is Entari, for peace? This is not who we are."

"No, Myra. Entari don't slaughter an entire continent of people, destroying ourselves in the process. We desire honor, and power; but there is no honor in what you wish to do, nor power, for anyone, if there will be no one left in the end but you."

In a swift motion, Myra gave a shout of anger, whipped a knife from her thigh-sheath and sliced wildly at Korr, who deflected at first with his sword, but its speed was too slow; he was forced to roll aside and slash at her to make her stop advancing. He struck her leg and she cried out and fell to the ground, struggling but unable to rise. She sat covering the gash with her hands, trying to block the bleeding.

Korr stood, sheathing his blade. Turning away from Myra he said to his clan, "Let us join the others."

Nej approached him, glancing at Myra. "Do what you have to do," Korr said, then moved to his troops, preparing to finish their journey. Nej knelt beside Myra, unwrapping the cloth from her arm. She slowly placed her hands before the crouched form and again harnessed the energy of the fragments. Myra was unable to do more than clutch the deep wound in her leg; her fragment felt the strength and pull of the others, and was gradually drawn free, floating among green wisps of energy to Nej.

Nej grimaced as the fragments connected, though she had grown accusomted to the process and now felt only a brief twinge upon the fusion. However, she was beginning to be afraid she might be unable to remove them; they had grown powerful. She buried her fears; she had a task to complete. She had convinced all the others, and they expected her to fulfill her promise. And there was one more fragment to go.

As Nej rose and stepped away from Myra, she was tempted to offer aid—she was a healer after all. But she suspected Myra would not want it. Myra was already tearing a strip of velvety cloth off her cloak and wrapping it around her wound, teeth gritted and jaw clenched. She pretended Nej wasn't there.

Sadly, Nej turned to follow the Entari toward their final destination.

As the Entari marched down the mountainside from the northeast, so too more individuals proceeded down the slopes from a more southeastern direction: the Zenura. They used the southern pass between mountains, which didn't require traveling high over them. They had been concerned about the potential for battle as well, especially with golems, but when they saw all those gathered, they realized there was no need to fear.

The last two clans arrived simultaneously. Vierux moved to the outside edge of those gathered to greet her people, Zuun following her. Nej saw and ran to them.

"Nej!" Zuun exclaimed with a grin as he hastened to meet her. They embraced happily, but Zuun's joy faded when saw the fragments affixed to her arm. "That doesn't look so good, Nej," he remarked, his brow furrowed in concern.

Vierux met with her guards and assured her people that all was well, thanking them for coming to see the event and the change that would renew their world. Then she joined Zuun and Nej, and Zuun introduced her.

Nej smiled. "Thank you for being so understanding," she said.

"Perhaps I, like others of our age, are ready for a change, as our elders were not," Vierux stated.

Nej nodded in agreement.

Then Vierux saw the fragments as well and gasped, taking hold of Nej's arm for a closer look. She shook her head. "No, this will not do. It will overtake you. They are unbelievably powerful. You must remove it immediately, if you can. Zuun and I can combine them safely inside here," she withdrew the small case which held the final fragment.

"This is my fragment. But I won't open it until you are free, or it will join the others and you'll never get rid of them."

Nej closed her eyes, concentrating deeply, trying to push the fragments away. She sensed they needed something to go to; some life to cling to. At last she let out a sigh. "I can't," she admitted, "Not like this. They must have somewhere else to go before they will leave." Vierux nodded, glancing at Zuun.

"Let's try the roots of the old tree.

"Well, what's left of them," Vierux added as she moved away, through the throngs of individuals surrounding the ancient remains.

The trio reached the spot, looking at it intently. Korr, Jyu, and Vai'shun joined them, coming together for the first time as several young H'toshen who desired change.

"How do we do it?" asked Vai'shun. Zuun turned and approached the golems.

"Can you fill this area with fertile earth and fresh water?" he asked. The golems murmured among themselves, then nodded. Jyu, Korr, and Vai'shun called for everyone to move back and make way as the golems circled the perimeter and began working: whirring and spinning, creating light and sound and eventually, earth and water. Nej's fragments glowed and energy seemed to flow toward the golems, aiding the process. H'nomi mages cast spells as well, focused winds that pushed the earth into the deep crevices. As the rifts began to fill, and the land around appear healthier with the fresh soil, Vierux placed her fragment, still encased, at the base of the old tree.

Nej gazed at the fragments in her arm, considering, then at last said, "No. They won't harm me. Give me the last fragment. I'll merge them, and then they will leave me on their own."

Vierux looked uncertainly at her. "You're sure?" she said. "I wouldn't trust an ancient seed—"

"We have to," Nej insisted. "Isn't that exactly what we're doing, by giving the tree a chance to grow and protect us again? The reason the tree was killed is because our ancestors no longer trusted it. They took matters into their own hands. And look where it brought us. Look how it destroyed us all. And look what wonderful things happen when we come together again."

Vierux gave a little sigh, looking away. She went and collected the seed, bringing it to Nej. Touching a combination of points on the metal box caused it to pop open, revealing the final, glowing fragment. This promptly rose up and combined with the others.

Everyone was forced to turn away, covering their eyes at the enormous glow that burst from Nej as the seed was completed. Nej could barely maintain focus; she tried to invoke healing upon it, ensuring its safe return to life, but felt too overwhelmed by its strength and the pain of it within her. Then at last the glow receded, and when the others turned back, Nej was holding the completed seed in her hands. She supposed it had used her energy, or her healing powers, to repair itself, and now, as requested, had left her, awaiting placement where it could grow.

"It's ready," she said breathlessly. "Now where do we plant it?"

Zuun held out his hand. Nej passed the seed to him, and he turned to Vierux.

"You made water and plants grow from a fragment. Can you make a tree grow from a seed?"

Vierux gave a sly smile.

"All you need is water and earth and sunlight," she said simply.

Jett approached them, and, touching the ground, created a mound of fresh, new earth. The lands around were looking full, the deep chasms nearly level again.

Vierux hesitantly took the seed and approached the burial spot.

Korr and Vai'shun took out their weapons and scraped out a hole in the dirt, into which Vierux placed the seed. They all knelt around and covered the seed with dirt. Vai'shun then opened a jug hanging at his side, and emptied his drinking water over the dirt. Korr and Jyu chuckled at this, and Vai'shun grinned back at them.

Everyone looked on with anticipation. But nothing happened.

"Maybe it needs a start?" Vierux suggested. "Some sort of magic to help it grow?"

"True, it certainly isn't a *normal* seed, maybe it needs something special," agreed Zuun.

Nej's brow furrowed. She recalled the words of Tiore, how it wasn't a seed at all, but a heart. She sighed deeply. The others turned to her. Nej shook her head.

"This won't work. It isn't what this seed needs.

"One of the leaders told me, the seed was the heart of the tree. I know now what must be done. I admit I had suspected, but hoped it wouldn't be so," she glanced at their faces.

"It's a sacrifice I'm prepared to make," she continued. "In fact I believe I'm the only one who can and must do it."

"Do what Nej?" Jyu said in alarm.

"Well," she forced a smile, to calm those around her. "Just watch," she invited them, her eyes glistening.

She gently uncovered the seed, then stood, holding it, in its place.

"Thank you all for what you've done; for making this possible," she said. "I'll watch over you forever now."

"Wait Nej, you can't," Zuun rushed forward, putting a hand on her arm. Her eyes met his.

"You might want to stand back," she whispered.

CHAPTER 15
Many, Many, Many Years Later

"What happened then?!" a little girl exclaimed excitedly, and with some alarm. Zuun chuckled, toying with his long white beard, then leaned forward, a hand gripping his ancient, gnarled walking staff. A group of young children surrounded him, listening to his tale. They sat in the lush green grass, just beyond the shade of the great Boikk tree. Warm sunlight engulfed them, and a gentle breeze stirred the air and grasses around them.

"The glow was blinding, as it had been when Nej combined the fragments and removed them from herself. And when we could see at last, glowing white roots and branches were growing, down and up—"

"But what happened to Nej?" another girl asked, a worried expression on her face.

Zuun took in a slow breath before answering. "We never saw her again, not as she was. Some say the tree used all her life force to create itself, and she died that day. But others say, she was transformed into the tree; not so different an idea, but a more pleasant one. That she is the tree: immortal, feeling our touch and hearing our laughter forever; keeping us safe.

"After all," he added, "doesn't the fruit of this tree cure any illness? And don't the leaves heal any wound"

"Yeah!" agreed his audience.

"Only Nej had such healing powers. She became something more than H'nomi, or H'toshen."

"But don't you miss her?" a young boy asked.

Again Zuun chuckled. "Don't I miss her," he repeated. "Don't I wish she'd grown old with the rest of us. And I'm sure that's what she wanted, too. But she did what she had to; what she alone could do; perhaps what she was meant to do. To bring us all together, and let the rest of us live in peace and harmony, with no more war or pain. And, in a way, she did grow old with us—and she will live on for much longer than any of us will.

"As long as we remember her and what she did, and keep what she is now, alive, she'll always be with us."

The children followed his gaze to the Boikk tree.